MYSTERY AT MELON FLATS

Frank Sutherland Davidson

OTHER BOOKS BY FRANK DAVIDSON

Frank Davidson is a graduate of the University of New England. Before concentrating on writing he had a career in teacher education at Sydney Teachers' College and Sydney University.

He is now a full-time writer of plays, short stories and novels. Recent works include "Bush Dreaming And Other Plays" [ISBN: 978-1-925909-02-9], and a lighthearted crime novel "The Coral Airlines Mystery" [ISBN: 978-1-4931-0186-3].

MYSTERY AT MELON FLATS

by

Frank Sutherland Davidson

PEGASUS PUBLISHING

Frank Sutherland Davidson

Mystery At Melon Flats

First Published in Australia in 2022

by
Frank Sutherland Davidson (1934)
Edited by Dr. Tracy Rockwell

Orders: pegasuspublishing@iinet.net.au

PO Box 980, Edgecliff, NSW, 2027

A CIP catalogue record for this book is available from the National Library of Australia.

ISBN: 978-1-925909-04-3

Printed on Demand by Ingram Lightning Source
www.ingramspark.com

Cover Image:
A white window framed stone house, from the North East of the USA (photographer unknown).

Contents

Frank Sutherland Davidson

CHAPTER 1

An unfortunate date and an unexpected invitation

It was Friday night and I'd taken Fiona out to dinner as usual. A new little restaurant just up the road from where I live in Balmain. Inexpensive – some would say cheap – the sort of place where they seem to pride themselves on letting you hear all the noise from the kitchen.

I remember I'd ordered "Steak au Poivre" underdone. When it arrived, Fiona, who'd ordered what appeared on the menu as "Fillet of Whiting Supreme avec Legumes Vert", gave one of her annoyingly sympathetic glances at the waiter; which he would have seen, if he'd been hovering. But he had urgent business back in the kitchen, from where the noise was deafening.

"He's preparing the Sauce Concrete for the Steamroller Pudding," I explained to Fiona above the racket. She looked unamused and most of the meal was eaten in silence except for what sounded like the crashing of gears, but was probably just a heavy wash-up.

Not that I wanted to talk anyway. It'd been a hell of a week at work, and I'd been looking forward to a bit of quiet when we got back to Fiona's place afterwards. That's what we usually did after a meal out on Fridays. But it was not to be.

We'd been lovers for a year. This dinner was really a kind of anniversary, although that didn't cross my mind until afterwards. After she'd dropped the bombshell.

"Darling," she'd suddenly said over her Strawberry Flambé Supreme, "I think we're seeing too much of each other."

This, mind you, was just as I'd taken a heavy bite of the "Torte Baghdad" that I'd been stupidly curious enough to order for sweets. My jaws were practically glued together.

"You'll ring me, of course," Fiona went on. "But we won't see each other. We'll call the other thing off for awhile."

"The other thing?" I managed to gasp, swallowing some lumps of the Torte Baghdad. "What other thing?"

"Sleeping together, you know," said Fiona, at her highest pitch. "It's been fun, of course. But getting to be too much of a habit, if you know what I mean. Now what I suggest is that we call a halt to sex. No sleeping together," she explained even more loudly, as though I were a foreigner or a pensioner, "until things sort themselves out."

"Sort themselves out?" I choked, "what do you mean sort themselves out?" I felt angry. It was just like Fiona, she always had some harebrained scheme.

"Come on," I said, as she took a sip of the Australian Sparkling I'd bought her, "what do you mean, until things sort themselves out? What things?"

Fiona had laid her spoon down on her empty plate. She has very delicate table manners but underneath her cool, smooth exterior there lurks the mentality of a cut snake. I was getting a good sample of it now.

"There are more things in heaven and earth than are dreamt of in your philosophy, Horace," she informed me primly.

I counted to six.

"In the first place," I said with suppressed assertion, "I asked you a specific question and instead of a specific answer I get one of Shakespeare's well-worn generalisations. And in the second, if you must quote 'Hamlet', at least quote it accurately. The guy's name was Horatio, not Horace," I had run out of breath, and quickly gulped some more wind. "And in the third place," I went on, quickly stifling an agonising belch, "none of this has any bearing at all on the crap you're handing me about not sleeping together. Why? What

11

have I done? Answer me!"

My assertion was getting less and less suppressed, and people were starting to look round. I knew that this was just what Fiona wanted, and tried to lower my voice, which made me choke.

"Darling! You eat too quickly!" she exclaimed in tones of solicitude that wouldn't have fooled a Hottentot. "Here – have a sip of my wine." And she poked her glass, fizzing like fury, right under my nose.

My mind was racing. To gain time, I took the glass she offered me and had a sip. The bubbles went right up my nose.

After I'd sneezed, I felt that I had the answer. I'd been too good to her. I'd given in too often. This time I wasn't going to. I took a deep breath.

"All right," I told her, adopting a gracious drawl, "I eat too quickly. So let's give it a rest. Whatever you say. And I'll ring you instead. You ring me too, of course." I signed to the waiter to bring the bill. "I don't feel like coffee, do you?"

"Darling!" she cried. "You are sweet. Of course you can ring me. I'll be at home tonight. We can start all over again on the telephone. Oh you are clever to know exactly what I mean. You'll see. And now, take me home."

"My place, or yours?" I said automatically. It didn't raise a laugh.

I tried to avoid the waiter's eye as he plonked the

bill down. I just shelled out quickly and told him to keep the change.

I didn't ring Fiona that night. Instead, after I'd left her at the door of her flat, I drove home to my terrace in Balmain and sat in the car for awhile, looking at the moonlight on the water at the bottom of the street. I had decided. She'd called it off – or as good as – and off it would stay. I wasn't giving in to any more crap. This was it.

As I went inside I noticed that there was a lot of mail poking out of the mailbox and I went through the letters. There were two of them in the same unfamiliar, old-fashioned handwriting that took my attention. I opened the thinner one. There was no date on it, and it seemed to have been laboriously copied out, like a handwritten circular:

Melon Flats
via Murrendebri

This is to inform you that your family is gathering at Melon Flats Come on Saturday 19 to the graveyard by the creek about 9 in the morning all who can

Not only was there no punctuation, there was no signature either. I opened the fatter one. Although the writing was different, and neater, it was only slightly more specific:

Melon Flats
via Murrendebri

The family gathering is on, we want to see all our kin

13

here in Melon Flats Saturday 19th. Bring any dietary requirements, Harry is roasting a sheep and we'll have home brew.

(signed) Muriel Chevally

This one included a roughly drawn map showing how to get from Murrendebri to Melon Flats, which seemed to be deep in the hills of the Cunjlebung Mountains, on a winding stream marked "Cunjle Creek". No doubt this was the creek where we were to meet in the graveyard.

I sat for awhile feeling astounded. My father had worked in the office of the Main Roads Board all his life, but I knew that his father, or his mother, I'd forgotten which, had come from somewhere up in the Cunjlebung Mountains, I'd never known where. As far as I'd known, my family consisted of my father, my sister, and my mother; and all of her family, of whom there seemed to be dozens, all in the Bank or in insurance offices or holding down important posts in business firms. As far as I knew, Dad had never had any family at all. Now, it seemed, I had some genuine hillbilly relation, living in a place I'd never heard of, inviting me to a reunion of a family I didn't know I had.

I didn't ring Fiona the next day, as I had got into the habit of doing, but as I waited for my frozen pizza to heat up that night I read Muriel Chevally's letters again. I tried to picture Muriel Chevally. She would be about sixty, I decided, with short grey hair cropped like a man's. Fat, wearing a shapeless faded print dress and gum-boots. And good at making "Home Brew". I got a tin of Fosters out of the fridge and snapped it open. I would go to this reunion at Melon Flats, I decided. It was too intriguing to miss. And I would ring Fiona straight away to tell her.

"Darling! You go!" she had said. "I'm having some of the girls from work over here on Saturday anyway. So you might as well enjoy yourself too!"

I hate that tone in her voice – as though she's got my mind open in front of her, reading it like a book. I could tell from the quiver of silence on the other end of the line that she was laughing. I couldn't see anything funny.

"And," I added, because I felt that the silence was undignified, "I'm going to accept it."

"Good for you, darling, "Fiona gasped. I could just see her, wiping the tears of mirth out of her eyes.

"When I get back," I continued, "I may ring you; or I may not. Goodbye." And I put the phone down. The pizza was ready. While I ate it, I got out the NRMA road map and worked out the best way to drive to Murrendebri.

CHAPTER 2

Something is strangely familiar ~ but why?

As the car hummed up the highway on the afternoon of Friday 16th, I tried to put the same distance between Fiona and myself that I was putting between myself and Sydney. In fact, as I thought about it, Fiona seemed altogether too much like Sydney – slick, superficial, a complex of drives and self-interests that pounded dangerously beneath that lovely exterior. Melon Flats would certainly be different.

I liked the sound of the name. Melon Flats. I turned it over in my mind. It had a feeling of ripe fertility about it. "Melon Flats", I mused into the setting sun.

For the first time, I wondered how Muriel Chevally had got my name and address. Had my sister Anne had an invitation too? I hadn't thought to ring her and ask. We're not always on the best of terms anyhow. That husband of hers is a real dag too.

I was approaching the last town in the valley, Murrendebri. On either side of the road were small farms, clustered along the banks of the creeks that run together to make the headwaters of the big river. An ivy-covered church with a square tower. Simple weatherboard houses with verandas, and washing hanging out the back. It looked charming; refreshing. Maybe Melon Flats would be like this too.

I wheeled into the best looking motel and sat for a moment staring into its office. It was a symphony of potted plants and plastic. I realised that it wasn't what I was looking for – it was smart, contemporary and could be anywhere from Collingwood to Chatswood. I revved up and swung out of the driveway, with a curious feeling that I was on horseback, not in a motor-car. A sort of time-warp seemed to descend on me. I didn't want to stay at a motel. The Royal Hotel was what I wanted.

Just up the road I saw it. An old hotel dating from the 19th century, two-storied, with a long balcony across the front decorated with uneven iron lace. As I got close, I could make out the name in faded letters on a sign above the balcony, "Royal Hotel". Well, every town has a Royal Hotel, or used to. All the same, I felt a bit uncanny. The facade looked more than just familiar; it was like seeing something that you've got a picture of, that you've looked at often, but only now seen the real thing. I shook off this feeling and pulled up at the curb.

It was cool under the wide balcony as I walked up the two worn stone steps into the hotel foyer and looked around for the office. For a minute, coming in like that out of the late afternoon sunlight, I thought there wasn't one. Then I could see the sign over one of the doorways, and walked in.

A nice-looking blonde woman was working at a desk. She looked up and smiled as I approached. I couldn't help smiling back.

"Have you got a room?" I asked.

She laughed. There was something about that laugh – I really can't explain it. "We've got several", she replied. "How long do you want it?"

"Just for tonight," I said; then, suddenly I wondered if there would be anywhere to stay in Melon Flats. "Well – I'm not sure yet about tomorrow night –" I figured I could always run back to town again if necessary.

She laughed again. She had a very nice mouth. "Just the one night then," she said. "Would you mind writing your name and address here?" She swung the register towards me and I filled it in. Roger Horsburgh, 18 Thorne Street, Balmain.

"I want the room second on the left," I said, as I threw down the pen. Oh my god, I thought, why did I say that?

"Oh yes, Number 2" she said, getting up. "Just

follow me."

Again I felt that peculiar sense of familiarity. I really felt a bit unsettled. Why had I asked for a particular room, in a hotel I had never been in before? I shook my head, trying to get the cotton-woolly feeling out of it. Travel fatigue, I decided.

"I hope your bar's open," I called as I followed her up the stairs.

"Oh, do you want a drink?" she called back to me.

"My word!" I said, stopping suddenly as I reached the wall of darkness at the top of the stairs. "The juice of the pomegranate lightens the heart for love," I whispered into the blackness.

Yes, that's what I said. Don't ask me what it meant. I just stood there in the dark, hearing that crashing sound that you hear in your ears when suddenly there is complete silence.

I was appalled. *Had I said that? Had I said that?*

There was a tinkle of laughter and a door opened, flooding light into the corridor.

"Number 2", said the blonde. I stumbled through the doorway into the room. She was checking the soap and towel at the old-fashioned wash-stand.

"It's too small!" I blurted out.

She stopped what she was doing and I could feel her looking at me. She didn't say anything, and I couldn't. I was wondering if I was losing my mind.

"Well…" she said uncertainly, after awhile, "we do have other rooms, if you…"

"No!" I was almost shouting. "No! This'll do fine! It's just what I wanted! Perfect! It's just that…"

I couldn't go on. How could I explain the feeling that had come over me? The feeling that the room should be bigger – the bed – a bigger one than this one – set out across the corner of the room, instead of against the wall like this? The canopy that should be over the bed… I shook my head but the feeling wouldn't go away.

"Just – that – there's no mosquito net" I managed to gulp, in an effort to get my head together.

She was looking at me curiously. No wonder. I must sound like a ratbag, I thought, as I floundered on, trying to sound normal.

"They, er, they attack me in the night", I said, "mosquitoes. I can't sleep unless I've got a net right over me."

This was a palpable lie and I was astonished all over again to hear myself saying it.

Fortunately, at this stage, the blonde took charge of the situation. She tinkled her laugh again and told me that mosquitoes were not expected in Murrendebri till February.

"I expect it's different in Sydney", she said. "But you won't have to worry here. The bathroom's at the end of the corridor there. Now, if you want a drink, I'll come down and serve you in the lounge. You must be tired, it's a hot day. Did you come straight up from Sydney?"

I could tell that she was doing a bit of detective work on me. No wonder, I thought, I must sound like a complete ratbag.

"Right!" I said, tossing my overnight bag onto the old wooden luggage stand. "Lead me to the watering hole. I've had a real cow of a trip."

"Yes," she said, "I thought you looked a bit strained. The traffic's terrible on a Friday, isn't it." She was chattering on as she led me down the stairs.

I was glad when we got into the lounge. It was empty and I asked her to pull me a Fosters.

"We don't have Fosters on tap but I can get you a cold can," she said briskly, sounding just like a competent nurse during tea-break in an operating theatre.

"No no," I said. "I'm not used to the country. Just a middy of whatever you've got. Make it a schooner."

While she was away getting the beer I'd asked for, I gave myself a talking to. You know – grow up, pull yourself together, that sort of thing. In no time, she was back with the schooner, and with a newspaper under her arm.

"Would you like to see the local paper?" she asked.

"Good-oh," I said, "thanks."

Have you ever seen those local newspapers? '*The Murrendebri Magpie*', this one was called. It was full of

21

chummy articles about golf and cricket and the Country Womens' Association. I read the lot. I wanted to get my mind off that feeling I'd had in Number 2 upstairs. Then, right there in front of me, was a name I knew. Muriel Chevally. Of course! There would be news of the family reunion in the *'Magpie'*. I eagerly read on.

'All Roads Lead to Melon Flats' the heading said. I felt my flesh creep, as though a cold chill had gone up my spine. *"Descendants of the Chevally brothers, original settlers in the Murrendebri district, are coming from far and wide to gather in the Melon Creek cemetery for a family reunion,"* it said.

Somehow I thought that whoever wrote that could have put it better, but I didn't want to laugh. I read on. *'Well-known Melon Flats descendant Miss Muriel Chevally is in charge of the organization, which will include a sports carnival and an address by Murrendebri Historian Mr Phineas Knottle. Miss Chevally and Mr Knottle hope that the gathering of so many members of this old Murrendebri family will throw some light on a long-standing mystery, the whereabouts of Amos Chevally's treasure, reputed to have been secreted by him before his death in 1888 and never discovered.'*

The blonde was still in the lounge, doing something at the other end of the room. "Excuse me," I called out, waving the *'Murrendebri Magpie'* in her direction, "have you ever heard of Melon Flats?"

She turned towards me and gave that laugh of hers. "Heard of it!" she exclaimed. "Why, I come from there! Used to, anyhow, when I was a kid. I've still got lots of relatives living up there. In fact," she said, coming down the room towards me, "I'm going up tomorrow.

There's a gathering of the family – we're all getting together for a family reunion."

I think my mouth probably fell open. "You're kidding," I said.

"Eh?" she said. "Why? No I'm not!" She looked really surprised.

"So you'll know Muriel Chevally," I said.

As I spoke, for the first time our eyes really met and I looked deeply into hers. They were beautiful. I was stunned.

"Ye-es," she said slowly, in a remote, almost absent-minded sort of way.

Then, suddenly snapping out of it, she looked directly back at me. "Why – you might be a relative too! That's why you look familiar! Is that why you're here? Is it?"

She was excited. I suddenly felt defenseless; not threatened, but vulnerable. Having something in common with a stranger would normally unsettle me but this was different.

"I've got a letter from someone called Muriel Chevally in my bag upstairs, though how she got my name and address beats me."

"So you are a relation! Gosh – how exciting! I don't recognize your name though. Which one are you descended from, Amos or Seth? Let me guess…"

"Hold on," I said, "I don't even know who Amos

and Seth are. I don't have a clue about where I fit in. What's it all about?"

Whether it was a reaction after driving all day, or maybe the beer was beginning to relax me, I don't know what it was, but a great feeling of sadness suddenly came over me. That I didn't fit in had never worried me – or perhaps it had, and I hadn't noticed. But now – the past seemed to rush over me like a wave, bringing all the insecurities I'd once felt and tried to put behind me. I hadn't had a home I'd ever fitted into, I didn't fit in with my sister and her crowd, it was obvious that I didn't fit in any more with Fiona, it was all too depressing. I wasn't going to let it get to me, though.

"Look," I said, "I don't know anything. I think my grandfather or maybe my grandmother came from up here, years ago, and I'd never even heard of Melon Flats until I got that letter. So tell me."

There seemed to be a curious dim silence in the lounge, a bit like what I imagine they mean when they speak of things being as silent as the tomb, although not far away were the raucous sounds you expect to hear from any nearby public bar.

"I'd better tell you my name," said the blonde, "seeing as how it seems we're cousins really. I'm June Chevally. There's a lot of us up this way, all descended from two brothers, Amos and Seth Chevally. That's what the reunion's about. We're getting together because it's 150 years since they came up here. At least, Seth came up then, and Amos came a few years later."

It sounded feasible – but I still felt remote from it. I felt strangely annoyed with myself. Blow it, I didn't want to fit in anywhere, anyway. For a moment, I wanted to just get in the car and wheel away up the highway, to anywhere, where how I fitted in wouldn't matter.

June's voice broke in.

"He started this hotel, she was saying. "Amos, that is. Just a shanty at first, then he built this place a couple of years later. It was the first stone building in Murrendebri. Then about forty years later, his son – my grandfather – built the balcony on and added to it and changed the name. Amos had called it the 'Royal Empire Hotel'. but Grandfather dropped the 'Empire' and just called it the 'Royal'.

"Funny name," I said. "Royal Empire."

"Oh, he was a funny old cove, by all accounts," said June.

"Was he indeed?" I said.

"He and Seth didn't get on," June continued, "they hated the sight of each other and never spoke."

Well, at least that was something I understood.

"I'm the same," I said. "Must be about two years since I've seen my sister Anne, let alone spoken to her."

But June had got into her stride and I could see she was determined to give me the definitive history of the whole family set-up; a regular soap-opera by the sound of it. Well, after all, I'd asked for it.

"The trouble was," she was saying, "that Seth had been sent out here from England. Some funny business that no-one knows the whole story of. But the scandal ruined the family so Amos went to India. Their father had been an inn-keeper in England apparently, and Amos opened a grog-shop for British soldiers in Bengal. That's how he made enough money to come and set up here."

"But if he didn't speak to Seth," I said, "what was the point of coming all the way up here? Surely he would have done better down around Camden, or up on the Hawkesbury, in those days, if he wanted to open a pub."

She shrugged.

"Who knows," she said. "But probably they loved to hate each other. You know how people are, especially in a family."

I wasn't sure that I knew what she was talking about, but I nodded. That gloomy feeling was coming over me again. I took a large sip of my beer.

What does it mean to love somebody, or to hate them for that matter – I thought of Fiona, but that made me feel even more depressed.

It was then, as I looked at June, that I noticed the engagement ring on her fourth finger.

As far as I can remember, at this stage a real confusion of feelings came over me. I do remember, though, that I thought, I'd better put this beer down. I don't want to get any more confused.

And then, somebody called to June from the front and she excused herself and went out into the foyer towards the office. I watched her go.

I've always found a sense of impermanence in women. It's been my experience that you can go with a woman for months, tell her you love her, sleep with her, get to rely on her even, and she'll turn round and kick you in the guts. I suppose I could have put that better, but that was how I felt, sitting on my own there in the lounge of the strangely familiar Royal Hotel.

I stared into my half-drunk schooner. It seemed to me that I had a lot to think about, but I couldn't quite get the thoughts together in my head.

It was just then that June returned.

"I know you'll have a map," she said, "but I'll be driving up to Melon Creek in the morning and if you like, you could follow my car."

I jumped to my feet. "Can't I give you a lift? In my car?" I said.

She laughed – that laugh again. "Oh no thanks," she said, "I'm really quite used to travelling on my own."

Somehow, the way she said it, it wasn't a put-down.

"Thanks for the offer," I said, "but I'll rely on my intuition – and Muriel's map."

"Good night then," said June, turning back

towards the foyer, "I hope to see you at the reunion!" And with that, she was gone.

Left alone in the lounge, I finished my beer and then, lured by the sounds of joviality coming from the bar, went off to find it. I would have just one more beer, I thought, to settle me down before I went upstairs to bed; I wasn't hungry and there would be a pub breakfast to look forward to in the morning.

In the bar there were about twenty guys and no room at the bar counter. The sound was deafening. I suddenly wanted to be alone, not in the middle of this mass of male humanity. So, I turned around, left the bar and headed for the stairs.

As I reached the top, and unlocked the door of No 2. I recalled that feeling I'd had in the afternoon when I'd been shown the room. Would it return, I wondered? I stepped inside. Everything was perfectly normal – that feeling must have been travel fatigue, just as I'd thought. I was ready for bed in minutes, and didn't know a thing until the next morning.

I'll spare you the details of what it was like trying to get a shower in the antique bathroom; sufficient to say that once I'd gone downstairs and found the hotel dining room, the breakfast they put on was fantastic.

Now the serious part of the day began. Armed with Muriel's map, I started the car and followed the directions, actually quite easily, until in about fifteen minutes I could see ahead of me what looked like a community hall, a little church, with a small graveyard behind it, one or two other buildings and a bridge over a creek. Yes – this was Melon Flats. There were a few cars parked near the church and I pulled up there and got out.

"Welcome to the Chevally Family Gathering!" yelled a large woman, coming towards me. "I'm Muriel, and let me guess, you'd be Roger from Sydney. Great to see you."

Well, Muriel was another surprise. She wasn't at all as I'd pictured her – she was one of those women that you think of as mature, rather than middle aged, and could have been anything from forty to fifty-five. Smartly dressed in tweeds, too, and not a gum boot in sight.

"Hi," I said. "Thanks for the map. Got here, no trouble. How did you track me down?"

"Oh, no trouble for our local historian," she yelled. "Phineas Knottle has quite a reputation for tracing people." She gazed fondly at a disheveled looking character lurking in the background. Bushy beard, wire-framed specs and one of those black duffel coats that must have survived from a 1950's Army Disposals store.

"Actually," I said, I was hoping to meet someone who I know will be here. Met her last night in Murrendebri."

"Aha!" exclaimed Muriel. "So you ran across June, at the Royal. Good. She can show you around," and with that, Muriel had turned on the heels of her stylish brogues and was off, back towards the Knottle

29

character.

Well, I thought, there's a bit of family resemblance – spend as little time as possible with people you don't know. This thought made me feel strangely at home. Maybe I would enjoy this family gathering more than I had expected to.

And there was June, getting out of her car, in which she had just pulled up and parked next to mine. I moved over there in an attempt to open the car door for her but I wasn't quick enough. She flashed me that smile of hers.

"Good morning," she smiled, "Roger – I presume it's all right to call you Roger, since we're not at the hotel?"

CHAPTER 3

A few more surprises

Somehow, seeing June again, I began to feel an unfamiliar sense of looking forward to something. I can only explain this by saying that up till then, for as long as I could remember, when something was coming up in my life I was never able to expect it to turn out well. That's probably why I got to be fairly good at my job as an insurance claims assessor – you'd be amazed how often people try to cheat on their insurance claims, and I'd got pretty good at sussing them out.

But feeling like that didn't make it any easier to make conversation and when I heard June say my name, Roger, for that first time, I was stumped as to how to reply to her.

Relief came from an unexpected quarter.

"Hello, June," shouted the voice of Muriel Chevally from where she and the Knottle bloke were standing some distance away. "Roger says he met you at the Royal so you might be able to take charge of him and show him around. The games will be starting in a few minutes – maybe he'd like to have a go at the sheaf-tossing".

It was on the tip of my tongue to shout back towards Muriel Chevally, something like "what sort of a tosser to you take me for," but fortunately the way June was smiling at me stopped that urge in its tracks and I suddenly realised that I was smiling back at her.

"Come on," she said, "let's go down to the sports ground and see what's going on."

I hadn't noticed it before, but down on the flat next to the creek there were people setting up activity areas, and I could see a fairly battered looking old ute parked there with somebody unloading sheaves of hay – presumably this was to be the sheaf-tossing I'd been threatened with.

"Sheaf-tossing," explained June as we made our way down to what was beginning to look like a sports ground, "is when you have to toss the sheaf over that bar they're putting up there, and the one who tosses the highest, wins."

I couldn't help it, my experience as a claims

assessor took over.

"But they're all different sheaves!" I exclaimed to June. "What about if some of them are lighter than others? Shouldn't they all be tossing the same sheaf? Or, at least, weigh them to make sure they're all the same?"

"Oh, I don't think anyone cares about that," June replied. "It's really only in good fun, you know."

Well, all I could think was, if I was running these games, I'd be putting some proper rules in place. But, as I reminded myself, I wasn't running them, and what did it matter anyway? What I really wanted was to enjoy the feeling it gave me to be spending some time with June. Suddenly I felt it easier to talk to her.

"June," I said, savouring the use of her name for the first time, "how come you're here on your own?"

We were striding along quite quickly and June was slightly ahead of me. She turned her head towards me and said "What do you mean, on my own?"

I don't know if you've ever realised while talking to someone that you've driven the conversation into a corner that you don't know how to escape from.

"Well," I said, thinking quickly, "I would guess that later on you'll be meeting your" – what word should I use? Boyfriend? Special guy? Fiancé? Future husband?

Before I could decide on what word to use, June had taken over, in that way she has. She stopped walking so suddenly that I almost bumped into her. But I didn't have time to apologise. In a gesture that I realise now was deliberate, she smoothed her hair back from her forehead, using her left hand. I noticed immediately. There was no engagement ring.

Now I was really flustered. Well – what can you do in a situation like that, but be honest. And I was. And, funnily enough, the words came quite easily.

"I'm sorry," I said, "but I thought that yesterday you had a ring on – you know, on the fourth finger – I thought you must be – well, you know –"

June laughed. "You thought I was engaged!" she hooted. "Engaged to be married! Well! I'm glad to see it worked. For you, anyway!" She was certainly enjoying the joke, whatever it was. I was still completely in the dark.

"Well, usually," I started to say, "when a girl's got a ring on that finger –" but June cut in.

We were standing quite still now, facing each other.

"I guess you don't know," she said. "I'd better explain something. I own the Royal, where you're staying. I not only manage it but I'm the licensee as well. It's really quite a big responsibility and, you know, we get all types coming in. Especially," she emphasised, "commercial travellers."

I could tell immediately where she was going with this.

"So," I said, "you wear a ring to show that you're not available."

"Well," she said, with a bit of a smile," I wouldn't have chosen to put it quite like that. But, essentially, yes, that's the idea."

"Brilliant," I said. "Had me fooled, for a start."

"Oh?" she said, in that remote sort of voice I'd heard earlier – while she looked into the middle distance as though she wasn't really interested in what I thought about anything.

I wanted to retrieve the situation but June wasn't giving me time to do anything of the sort.

"Come on," she said, "I can see that they're setting up the archery. That might suit you, more than sheaf-tossing."

"Archery!" I exclaimed. "How did you people here in Melon Flats l get interested in something exotic like that?"

"Well," said June, "to tell you the truth, it's a bit of a mystery. But as far as I know, my ancestor Amos – he was my great-grandfather, you know – or, at least, he was one of them – brought it with him when he came on here from India. It's always been a bit of a competition, between the Amos descendants and the Seth descendants – although, like me, some of us are descended from both of them – so it's a bit confusing." She laughed then, and I marveled again at the way she illuminated whatever she was saying with her obvious good nature, and – yes – I was recognising it now – her simple beauty.

But now I wanted to find out more.

"So," I said, "you're descended from both this Amos guy, and this Seth guy, the brother he never spoke to. How does that work?"

"Oh look," said June, "it's all a bit complex. Why don't you wait until this evening, when Muriel's – friend – the historian – will be giving a talk on the family, up at the homestead?"

"You don't mean that Knottle character, do you?" I asked.

"Well, yes," she replied. I couldn't help noticing a note of caution in her voice.

"Don't tell me he's a relative too," I said.

"Oh, no," June replied – "he isn't. It's just that Muriel – how shall I put it – well, she's a bit besotted by him."

"Ah," I said – and I regretted it the moment the words were out of my mouth – "they're on together, are they."

June gave me a level look, and paused briefly before she answered.

"If you must put it like that," she said.

I couldn't think of anything to say in reply to that and there was silence for a while as we walked on towards the sports ground. There was a guy who seemed to be putting up one of those targets on a stand, and another assembling some bundles of what looked like arrows.

This, I thought, will be the archery competition. Funny sort of sport to have here in the Australian bush.

"You said that Amos brought archery with him from India," I said to June, as we slowed down on reaching the archery area. "Why would he have wanted to do that?"

June smiled that smile of hers. "I can see I'll have to tell you a bit more about the family history," she said, "as much as I know of it, anyway."

"Yes please," I said. I just wanted to hear her talking to me, it didn't matter particularly what the conversation was about. But, as I realised later, the information June was giving me would turn out to be important.

"Well," she said, "from what I can gather, Amos and Seth came from somewhere in Staffordshire in England, where their father was an inn-keeper."

"Same as you!" I chipped in.

She laughed. "Yes, I suppose you could say, it's in the blood," she said. "All I know is, that Seth got into some sort of trouble and got himself arrested for stealing a horse."

"So that's how he ended up here!" I exclaimed. "Did they send him out here as a convict!"

"That's exactly it," said June. "He was only very young – no older than seventeen or eighteen – but they gave him a sentence of seven years, which he served somewhere up in this district, and when it was over, he was able to take up some land. That's how he got

37

started, and he ended up owning a fair bit around here, including the house you'll see tonight when we have Muriel's tour and the address from Phineas Knottle."

"Sounds like a good story," I said. I felt a bit chuffed, to hear a family story that seemed to have turned out well.

"Yes," said June, "but the best part of it is, that the girl he was keen on in England came out to New South Wales as an assisted migrant, found out where he was, and got work in a household up this way, and they ended up getting married and living here." She waved her arm around the area we were standing on.

That gave me a real pause. I didn't say anything, but I thought, I bet none of the girlfriends I've had would have done anything like that for me. If I'd been stupid enough to steal a horse in the first place, that is.

"What did he have to go and steal a horse for?" I asked June.

"I'm not sure about that," she replied. "But I heard from Muriel that Mr Knottle has some new information on the family, so perhaps we may possibly find out tonight."

The prospect of having to sit down and listen to whatever the Knottle character intended to burble on about was not exactly what I had in mind for the evening, but, as I reminded myself, I was not in charge of these events and what I should do was try to go with the flow – it had worked so far, and I hoped it would continue. Despite the fact that June and I were apparently related

– however distantly – I was feeling a real potential connection with her, and who knew what this feeling might lead to.

Now, one of the archery guys – the one who was looking after the arrows – came up to us.

He was holding a whole sheaf of arrows in one hand, and a bow for shooting them in the other. "Hello, June," he said.

"Hello, Ralph," she replied; then she turned and said to me, "Roger, this is our cousin Ralph Chevally." I was beginning to recognise a few family characteristics, and although June was blonde and this guy Ralph had very dark hair, I could see a kind of similarity in the shapes of their faces.

Ralph freed his right hand by tucking the bow he was carrying under his left arm, and I shook hands with him.

"Roger was just asking me why Amos brought archery with him from India," June said. "Do you know the background?"

"Yeah, well a bit," drawled Ralph. I could tell that he wasn't going to be able to say much about it, but what he did say proved important to the whole picture of the family that a I was slowly forming in the back of my mind.

"It was his wife," said Ralph. And with this enigmatic statement, he fell silent and was obviously not going to be able to add any more to the information.

"You mean, his wife did archery as a sport?" I asked.

"I guess so," said Ralph. "That's what they say."

I didn't like to ask Ralph who "they" were, but June stepped up to the mark.

"I think," she said, "that Muriel's — friend — Mr Knottle — might have the answer to that. We're going to hear from him tonight, before the barbecue."

"Struth," drawled Ralph. "I'll be ready for a pint or two of the Amos home brew, after having to listen to old Knottle," he said.

"Home brew!" I exclaimed. "Ah! That'll be the home brew that was mentioned in Muriel's note that she sent out. The second one," I added. I was starting to feel interested in the story of Amos and his venture into India. So I asked, "do you know, did Amos bring his home brew recipe with him from India as well as his archery?"

It was June who answered my question. After all, she was running a hotel, and might have been expected to know the answer.

"We think he did bring his recipe with him," she said. "And it's been handed down through the family ever since."

"What you might call a treasured inheritance," I said, thinking of the mention of treasure in the 'Murrendebri Magpie' article I'd read the night before.

"Oh, there've been changes over the years to the way it's made," said June, "what they make today probably isn't at all like what Amos made originally. For a start, he wouldn't have been able to get the same ingredients here, as he would've in India."

Ralph had obviously had enough of this talk about Amos's home brew recipe. "Want to have a go at the target?" he asked me, as he held out his sheaf of arrows as though offering me to pick one of them.

"Well –" I said reluctantly, "I've never tried to shoot an arrow before, so I don't think –"

"Oh, go on!" exclaimed June. "After all, you're probably an Amos descendant, like Ralph and me. Just what would Amos think, if he knew you didn't want to shoot one of his arrows?"

"I'd guess he wouldn't give a –" I started. I was just about to say "a rat's arse", but remembering how June had shown a distaste for a couple of racy remarks I'd already made that morning, I stopped myself just in time.

"A pig's bottom?" supplied Ralph, as he grinned helpfully. I quickly took one of his arrows and he showed me how to fit it to the bow. I drew back the string on the bow and let fly.

Of course, the arrow didn't land anywhere near the target, but it narrowly missed the guy who had been putting the target up.

"Shit!" he yelled at us. "Bugger off, Ralph."

"I think," said June, "it's time we moved on. Look, over there is where they're just starting the three-legged race." She pointed in the other direction and, taking my arm, she led me away. I was really thrilled to feel the pressure of her hand on my arm but I didn't like to say so in case she took it away. Which she did anyway, telling me that she'd taken part in the three-legged race ever since she had been growing up here at Melon Flats.

Suddenly I had an idea.

"Why don't we go in it, I said. "You and me."

June looked at me but I couldn't read her reaction.

"The three-legged race," I said.

June gave me a smile.

"Don't you think you're a bit old for it?" she said. It was then that I noticed that the people lining up at the starting line were all kids. Round about the ages of six or more, by the look of them.

I tell you, I'm not easily embarrassed, but that did it, I could tell by the flush I felt in my face that I'd gone red. And, to make matters worse, June was giving me that look again, as though she was trying to figure out something about me.

There's no doubt about her, she knows how to smooth over a difficult situation.

"I think," she said, "that you're starting to feel at home here, in the old family environment." And she gave my arm a squeeze. I couldn't think of anything to reply, which, when I think about it now, was probably just as well.

"Now. I know that Muriel wants to have a word with you," she said, "so why don't we go and find her, and she can answer any questions you have about where you fit into the family."

"I'd rather stay with you," I blurted out. June gave me a smile that set my heart racing.

"We can meet up again, for the tour of the homestead," she informed me. "Come on. Muriel is up there at the registration table." She pointed up the hill, and sure enough, there was Muriel, seated at a table covered with what looked like name tags. Fortunately, there was no sign of the Knottle person.

There was nothing else for it, I allowed June to lead me up to Muriel's table.

"Aha!" Muriel shouted as we approached. "I see you've taken Roger in hand, June. You can leave him to me now. Take a seat, Roger, and I'll sort you out."

I felt my gorge rising but, mindful of June standing there, I refrained from telling Muriel what I thought of being sorted out by her and meekly took the chair she indicated.

"See you later, Roger," said June; and she turned, and I watched her walk away with that effortless grace she always has.

"Now then, Roger," said Muriel, clearing her throat, as though she was in a shipping channel somewhere issuing a fog warning, "who was your father."

Instead of saying something like "what business is it of yours", as I would have normally, I counted to six. That calmed me sufficiently to be able to say, with relative civility, "Just a minute. I need to know who you are first."

"What!" exploded Muriel. "Hasn't anybody told you? I'm Matron Muriel Chevally, one of the senior Seth descendants in this family, and I run a respite nursing home in Willow Vale. Of which," she added in magisterial tones, "I am the proprietor."

"Willow Vale. Why, that's the next town up the highway," I said.

"Well, at least you seem to know where you are, if not who you are," said Muriel sarcastically. She consulted a sheaf of notes that she had in front of her. "It seems from this," she said, "that you're descended from Amos's eldest daughter, Margery, who married a free settler and had a daughter who married a Horsburgh."

"Sounds right," I said. "Great. That means," I said, leaning back in the chair, "that I'm descended from a free settler. Not a convict."

Muriel bridled noticeably, and I saw, not without satisfaction, that my shot had gone home.

"If," she said, giving me a steely look, "you are referring to Seth's transportation for something he was innocent of, you are poking the wrong end of the stick up the matter."

I could see that she was on the defensive, and I smiled condescendingly.

"Furthermore," Muriel went on, "just wait for tonight's lecture from Phineas, and you might be in for an unpleasant surprise."

"Anyhow," I said, from what you say, I'm an Amos descendant, so that's that."

"Yes," said Muriel, "and there'll be more on that subject in tonight's lecture. Now, why don't you go off, have a wander round, and try not to offend anyone else. Here, take your name badge."

She handed me a home-made identity badge with my name on it, which I pinned to the front of my shirt.

By this time it was getting on towards the lunch hour and I made my way down to where a sausage sizzle was in progress. I couldn't see June anywhere, but I took an interest in watching everyone else and sat down under a tree, with a huge sausage sandwich smothered in tomato sauce, to enjoy the golden afternoon sun.

Finishing the sandwich, I was just relaxing, watching the family crowd mill about, and thinking that this country life was more enjoyable than I'd expected, when up shambled the figure of Muriel's boyfriend, the Knottle character. I tried to ignore him but it didn't work.

"Hello," he said. "I believe that you're Roger Horsburgh." I realised that it was useless trying to throw him off the scent, so I nodded.

"Did you know that you've got an Indian ancestor?" he asked me.

This information struck me as so ludicrous that I laughed out loud. "Pull the other leg, it whistles," I chortled.

"Oh well," he sighed, "I suppose there's none so blind as those who don't want to see," and off he went, shaking his head.

Strange as this incident was, as I sat there I couldn't help puzzling over it. But suddenly, the sight of June coming towards me pushed everything else out of my mind.

"Hi!" she said. "I was wondering where you'd got to, Muriel said you were incorrigible and you went off in a huff, so I thought I'd better find you to see that you're all right."

"Never felt better," I informed her, "especially seeing you," I added.

June gave me that smile of hers, and then said "I thought you might like to come up and have an early look at the homestead, where we're going to have Muriel's friend Mr Knottle's lecture, and then a barbecue. Our cousin Harry, who owns the place now, is getting ready to roast a whole sheep, to feed everybody."

"Oh!" I said, as one more item from Muriel's second note fell into place for me. "A whole sheep! And home brew to go with it! Sounds like quite a feast."

"Yes," said June, "country hospitality. Come on,

it's a bit of a walk."

I readily fell into step beside her, and we set out. We crossed the creek on a little wooden footbridge and started to climb the slope beyond it. There was a gravel drive leading through the trees and we followed that.

"It was Seth's wife, Agnes, who decided on the site for the house," said June, as we walked.

"Ah!" I said. You told me about her. Followed him out here from England. Sounds like true love."

I was a bit startled to hear myself saying that. True love was not exactly my normal topic of conversation. But apparently it was just the sort of thing that June wanted to hear.

"Doesn't it just!" she exclaimed. "I've always been especially proud of Agnes, my great-grandmother."

The idea of being proud of your ancestors was also a new idea to me, and I pondered it a bit as we walked. "I suppose," I said, "if you've got an ancestor you're proud of, it's probably ten to one that you've also got another one somewhere that you're not particularly proud of."

"Oh," said June, "you don't have to go very far to see the truth of that." As she said this she had such a solemn look that I thought to myself, this is something I don't want to pursue, it could be a real downer by the look on June's face, and I wanted anything but that.

"What's so special about this house, anyway?" I asked.

"Well," said June, "it was part of that awful rivalry between the brothers that I've told you about."

"Yes, but I haven't heard what the cause of that was," I replied.

"I can't tell you what the cause was, except that apparently it had something to do with what happened in England," June said. "But, according to Muriel, we're going to get some insight into it when Mr Knottle gives his talk at the homestead. So we really haven't much time to wait."

I groaned inwardly at the thought of spending an hour or so listening to Knottle, but I didn't say anything and it was just at that moment that we turned a corner of the driveway and I could see in front of us the quite striking facade of what looked from here like a small but very handsome colonial two-storied mansion.

CHAPTER 4

Mr Knottle's talk is not so boring after all

The sight of the house was so unexpected that I stopped in my tracks. When I'd set out from Sydney to find the family that I had suddenly been made aware of, I never expected to find anything so solid and – I had to say the word to myself as I gazed at the building in front of me – so impressive. And to think that a member of my family – sent to New South Wales as a convict, for whatever reason – had achieved this just astonished me.

"So this is the house that Seth built," I finally remarked, as I stood with June looking towards the house.

"Well, yes," she replied, "but of course it was the centrepiece of quite a substantial pastoral holding. In fact, Seth eventually held the title of this whole valley. Over ten thousand acres, so I'm told."

I couldn't help myself. "Bloody hell," I burst out, "the guy was a plutocrat!"

"I think at the time he was just called a squatter," June said. "In fact, that was part of the difficulty between him and Amos."

"How so? " I asked.

"Well," said June, "Amos came to New South Wales from India expecting to be able to lord it over his younger brother, who had disgraced the family by being sentenced to deportation. But what he found instead, was in fact a successful landed proprietor, with assets far surpassing whatever Amos had brought with him from his years in India."

I don't know how to explain it, but it was then that I felt what I can only describe as a psychic jolt. I suddenly felt flooding through me the jealous anger that Amos, my great-grandfather, would have felt, on coming up here from the settled regions around Sydney, to find out what had happened to his convicted younger brother. And instead of finding whatever he had expected – a bark hut, perhaps – he had found – this.

June interrupted my reverie "Let's go in," she said," I'll show you through the house quickly before Muriel comes up. Then you won't have to suffer through her tour."

"Thanks, I'd like to see it," I said. "But doesn't somebody live here?"

"Oh yes," said June, "Harry and his family. You'll probably see them out the back getting the barbecue ready. They won't mind us looking through."

Well, I thought to myself, I hope Harry's got suitable insurance. I was reminded of one of the claims I'd recently had to deal with – the owner had written 'Great-aunt Ethel came to visit, tripped over the carpet breaking her foot which shattered the dining room window'. You get a lot of funny claims like that in the insurance business.

"How many rooms are there?" I asked June, as we stepped up onto the front porch

"Not a lot, really," she said, as we passed through the open front door into a narrow hallway. "On the ground floor there's just the sitting room – on the right, and the dining room here on the left." We looked briefly into both rooms, then June led me to the end of the hallway where a narrow staircase led to the floor above. "All the bedrooms are up there," she said. "Just four of them, I think."

"So despite the fact that it's two-storied, it's really no bigger than an ordinary house," I said.

"Yes, but I think, at the time, it was a statement," she replied.

"Designed to impress," I said.

"I think the design simply reflected some of

the houses great-grandmother Agnes would have remembered in England," said June. "They weren't all big manor houses. And don't forget, the working parts of the house are all over here, built separately," and she pointed at what lay across the courtyard – a single storied block which was obviously the kitchen, laundry, store rooms and all that sort of thing.

"That would have been because of the danger of having a fire," I said. "That's why in the old days they built the kitchen separately."

"You're right!" said June.

"Well," I said, "I'm not in the insurance business for nothing."

It was just then that I heard the voice of Muriel Chevally, in the distance but perfectly audible. She was chivying along a handful of people, obviously new recruits to the family gatherings who hadn't known what they were letting themselves in for.

"Come along everybody, keep up," she was yelling.

June had obviously heard her too. "Come and meet Harry," she said, and we walked to the back of the kitchen block, well out of the way of Muriel's tour, and right where a whole sheep's carcass was slowly turning on a spit over an open fireplace.

Harry was a tall, well-built guy in his thirties, with an open, honest face that I liked the look of. "G'day, Roger," he said. "Heard you were coming. Got the news from the foghorn."

June giggled. "That's what some of us call Muriel," she said. "It's a bit cruel, really…"

"…but accurate," Harry interrupted.

"Anyway," June said to Harry," I wondered if we could offer to give you a bit of a hand setting up for the barbecue?"

"Thanks, Cuz," said Harry. "You could help the kids get the trestle tables out. They're stacked in the storeroom behind the laundry."

Harry's three children appeared then, and between us all we got the tables set up and laid out with the plates and cutlery the kids brought from the kitchen.

"Merle will put out the salads while you two go and listen to the Knottle version of the family history," Harry said to us.

"Merle is Harry's wife," June explained. "She's a local girl, but not related to the family."

"Fresh blood," grinned Harry. "Anyway, who knows – Knottle might have some new information after all."

"Muriel definitely seems to think so," said June. "Let's go in, I can hear everyone arriving."

"Enjoy!" laughed Harry, as he turned his attention to the roasting sheep.

In the sitting room, Harry's kids were busy bringing in spare chairs from the dining room and elsewhere and arranging them in rows. Muriel was busy too, setting up a table at the front, and plugging in a microphone. I tried to draw June's attention to a two-seater couch that I would have liked to share with her, but she had her own ideas and shepherded me to the front row. "I don't want to miss any of Mr Knottle's revelations," she said.

It was then that I thought of the pocket recorder I always carry. It has often been useful when I've had to point out to people claiming an insurance payout, that they haven't always told the same story twice. Maybe Knottle might make a few self-contradictory statements and if so, I could impress June afterwards by pointing them out to her.

By now the family – those of them who had come up to listen to the Knottle talk – had settled themselves on the chairs, although Harry's kids and a few other younger ones who didn't have seats were settled on the floor at the back of the room. At the front, Muriel grasped the microphone and glared at her audience.

"I want you all to give a big welcome to our guest speaker, Mr Phineas Knottle," she ordered us. "He has devoted a lot of his time to uncovering some previously unknown details about our family, and he has generously agreed to share his findings with us tonight."

"He's getting a free feed for his trouble," a man's voice in the row behind me muttered. I stifled a laugh and looked sideways at June, who had turned in her seat to glare at the interruption.

"Shh!" she whispered. I busied myself turning on my little recorder and prepared to hold it discreetly in front of me, ready to capture the deathless words of Phineas Knottle.

But where was he?

"Phineas!" yelled Muriel into her microphone. "You can come in now. We're all ready for you." For a minute nothing happened and then the door from the hallway slowly opened and Phineas Knottle shambled up to the table and took the microphone that Muriel thrust in front of him. She then seated herself in the chair at his side. Rather like someone preparing to chair a board meeting, I thought to myself.

"Welcome our speaker," Muriel commanded, as she clapped her hands vigorously.

"Thank you, thank you, thank you,' mumbled Knottle into the microphone.

"I shall commence my address," he said, "by painting a picture of the Chevally family before their emigration."

"Deportation, don't you mean?" interrupted a voice from the back of the room.

Muriel was on her feet in an instant, and she didn't need the microphone. "You Amos descendants," she shouted, "needn't be so smug. Wait till you hear what Phineas has to say about you."

That made me sit up. For the first time, I felt a bond of sympathy with my fellow Amos descendants – whoever they were, apart from June, who had already said that she shared descent from both the brothers. The atmosphere had become volatile and I was beginning to quite enjoy it.

Knottle had spread out a bulky sheaf of papers on the table. "I have been fortunate," he said, "to have made contact with two family sources in Staffordshire, England. This is where the Chevally family lived – before – before" he faltered.

"Before they came here," supplied Muriel.

"Yes yes," Knottle resumed, "before they came here."

Now an expectant hush had come over the room and from here on, I am relying on my recording of Knottle's talk, which was mostly audible except when he mumbled or waved the microphone about as he tried to illustrate a point. These passages I have left out; I have also left out the occasional comments thrown at us by Muriel. So, what follows is essentially what Knottle presented.

"The first of these sources," he began, "is the Summerfield Family History Society, to whose Honorary Secretary, Miss Christobel Fotheringham, I am deeply indebted."

I know I said I was leaving out Muriel's intrusions but I can't resist reporting the look of scowling disapproval she gave Knottle on hearing of his indebtedness to Miss Fotheringham. But to continue Knottle's presentation:

"Summerfield is a small village in Staffordshire dating from medieval times and clustered around an ancient manor of the same name – an old house," and here Knottle gazed vaguely around the sitting room, "an old house in some ways not unlike this one."

There were one or two gasps heard at this point and I couldn't help noticing June's smile as she took in the news; no doubt she was thinking again of her great-grandmother Agnes, who had left home to follow Seth to an unknown future on the other side of the world, and had ended up mistress of a house reminiscent of one she would probably have visited as a child.

"Miss Fotheringham," Knottle continued, "whom I was able to meet in person on my recent visit to Staffordshire, confirmed that the Chevally boys, Amos and Seth, were indeed the sons of the village inn-keeper, Joseph Chevally. She was also able to give me previously unknown details of the younger brother, Seth's… er… er "

There was a perceptible pause here. For the sake of accuracy I do have to include Muriel's contribution to the Knottle research.

After his pause had become too lengthy to ignore, Muriel intervened. "Seth's misfortune," she stated, firmly emphasising the word 'misfortune' while at the same time glaring at the audience in case any Amos descendant should have the audacity to contradict her.

"Er – yes," continued Knottle, "his – er – misfortune." With an apologetic look in Muriel's direction he cleared his throat and proceeded bravely onwards.

"Seth at the time," said Knottle, "had a job at the local Summerfield livery stables. That," he explained, as though speaking to an assembly of the retarded, "was a place that kept horses for hire, if any of the local landowners needed more horses than they had in their own stables. For instance," he expanded, "if one of the annual events such as a meet was coming up."

"A what?" interjected a voice from the back of the room.

"I think," said Knottle, "that today we would call it a race meeting."

"Ar!" said the interjector. "You mean like the Murrendebri Cup."

"Just so," Knottle replied. "A race meeting with a lot of local prestige attached to it."

Here followed a lot of commotion, out of which I could just detect Muriel calling for order, before things quietened down and Knottle continued.

"According to local reports, made available to me by – Miss Fotheringham –" Knottle paused briefly to direct a conciliatory glance at Muriel, "Seth although only sixteen or seventeen years of age had already demonstrated noticeable capability as a horseman. It would have been usual," he continued, "for one of the local landowners to have engaged him as a rider to take part in the meet. But that didn't happen."

I remember, I was really wrapped up in the story now, and could hardly stop myself from calling out

"Why not?"

But somebody else, again from the back of the room, did it for me. "Why not?" he yelled.

After a brief period of commotion, Knottle's voice could be heard supplying an answer.

"Because," he stated, "and – mind you – I am relying here on the findings of the Family Historical Society that I mentioned – yes, this is not something that I have personally discovered – it is the work of dedicated historians in Staffordshire – or I should say, the dedication of one dedicated historian in particular – whose name I have already mentioned –"

At this point there was a considerable outburst from the audience and listening to the recording today I can distinguish a few words such as "get on with it", and a few other interjections such as "pull your finger out" that I don't think it's necessary to include. Eventually, Muriel managed to subdue the commotion and Knottle continued.

"It is now clear," he stated, "that the proprietor of the livery stables was offered a bribe to prevent Seth from riding a horse, widely tipped to win the main race at the meet, a horse owned by a local farmer whose daughter – a girl by the name of Agnes – Seth was known to have a romantic association with."

I can't really describe to you how this statement made me feel. I knew immediately that the Agnes that Knottle had referred to was June's great-grandmother. What a story this was becoming!

"Now," Knottle resumed, "the question to be decided is, who would want Seth not to ride in that meet, and why."

A rustle of excited comment echoed round the room until Muriel restored order and Knottle continued.

"It's quite a complicated story," he commenced, "and I'm not sure that I – I mean, Miss Fotheringham – has really managed to get to the bottom of it. But, fortunately, and with thanks again to the good office of Miss Fotheringham, I have managed to also personally meet and conduct a correspondence with a sympathetic descendant of the local squirarchy and this has thrown light on what perhaps lay at the root of the problem."

Here, Knottle availed himself of a glass of water, while various comments in the room can be heard, none of which are worth reporting. It is worth saying though, that as soon as Knottle started to speak again, there was complete silence from the audience as everyone – including me – leaned forward to hear the next revelation. It took Knottle quite a while to get to the point but eventually he did.

"Thanks to Miss Fotheringham," he stated, "I was encouraged to make contact with the Honourable Basil Summerfield, a direct descendant of the long line of squires who have owned Summerfield House since medieval times. According to several meetings and some letters which I have managed to exchange with the Honourable Basil, I learned that the story of Seth Chevally is well known in that family."

There were a few groans of impatience at this point, which led Knottle into a long and boring description of how, through his meeting with that Miss Fotheringham he'd kept mentioning, he had come to engage in correspondence with this Basil bloke. I'm going to leave all this out as it doesn't help with the story.

In fact, from here on I'm going to emphasise the main points of Knottle's presentation. This might make it easier to understand how things eventually turned out for the Chevally brothers in New South Wales.

In doing this, the story is not going to be very kind to my great-grandfather Amos, but after all, you can't help who you're descended from, so what does it matter. In fact, when I talked this over later with June, what she said really helped me to come to terms with it.

"Don't forget," she said, "that Seth and Amos had the same parents. And so you're descended from their parents too, not just from Amos, so you've got them to thank for all the good qualities you've got." That was the first time that June had given me what you could call a nod of approval, and I've never forgotten it.

Well, to get back to Knottle's revelations.

"I have carefully reviewed the notes I have made from meetings with, and letters I received from, the Honourable Basil," he droned.

"From what he has imparted to me, there was no doubt in the mind of the Summerfield squire of the time – a somewhat remote ancestor of the Honourable Basil – that if the farmer's horse were to run, it would be

61

the winner. Especially," Knottle emphasised, "with the skilled rider Seth Chevally in the saddle. Therefore," he said, "the squire devised a devious plan."

At this point Knottle took another sip of water – he was obviously not used to public speaking and when he went to put his glass down on the table I still have on my recorder the sound it made when he missed the table and the glass crashed to the floor and smashed into pieces. At this point I turned the recorder off until things had settled down and Muriel had mopped up the mess.

I missed the first few words of Knottle's resumed speech as I was occupied in discreetly turning my recorder back on but I didn't miss anything of importance. What did come next was a bit of an eye-opener though.

"According to the Honourable Basil," he was saying, "mind you, he had no documentation, I am only reporting hearsay…" and Knottle then embarked on a lengthy explanation of what the word hearsay means.

"Oh Gawd," muttered the man behind me, "too much Say, and not enough Hear."

Unfortunately, this time the guy's voice was louder and his comment reached the ears of Muriel so we had to wait while he was chastised for interrupting. With this accomplished, Muriel turned to Knottle and said in what I can only describe as an attempt at honeyed tones, "Do go on, Phineas, I am sure that the Amos descendants here tonight will be especially interested."

"Well – well – I'm not sure about that…" Knottle stuttered but he went on anyway. "I was telling you about the squire's devious plan. He offered the farmer a sum of money to withdraw his horse from the race meeting."

This gave me a funny sort of personal insight into the story. More than once I've been offered a little 'present' if I would agree to some obviously inflated insurance claim, so I knew immediately what that squire was up to.

"Of course," Knottle went on, "he couldn't be seen to be doing this himself, so he needed an intermediary." This struck a note with me too. Just like some of the people I've had to deal with, I thought.

"Now," said Knottle, "it so happened that the farmer had a very attractive daughter. Apparently she was widely admired and had even caught the attention of the squire's younger brother who, from what I could gather, had held a commission in the Bengal Lancers for a number of years and was home on furlough."

Typical upper-class British bastard, I thought to myself, I hope she had the sense to send him packing.

"That situation," said Knottle, "was a little complicated by the fact that the squire's brother already had a domestic arrangement in India."

Even worse, I thought – the randy bastard comes home and leaves the lady wife to cope with the Indian climate while he rocks around trying to seduce the local farmer's daughter.

"I'm not sure," said Knottle, in a rather hesitant manner, "that I'm able to put the following information as discreetly as I would like to."

At this point, Muriel couldn't contain herself. She burst out, "Go on Phineas, let them have it," and she settled back in her chair as though she was some company chairman just about to announce a successful take-over bid.

No doubt encouraged by this support, Knottle continued. "As it happened," he said, "the farmer's daughter was admired not only by Seth Chevally but also by his elder brother, Amos."

I remember at this point that I felt something like a chill running down my spine. Bloody hell, I thought, they both wanted the same girl. And it was obvious, by what she had done later, that Agnes clearly was in love with Seth, not Amos.

"Yes," Knottle went on, "the squire engaged Amos Chevally to negotiate a price with the farmer for him to withdraw his horse from the meet. This of course meant that Seth Chevally was no longer able to ride in the race that he had expected to."

Suddenly I realised as I listened that this odd family I had stumbled across all made sense. Two brothers – same girl – she chooses one, and the brothers never speak to each other again. Or so it seemed to me at the time. No wonder Amos turned into a twisted, bitter old guy, I thought, not only jealous but bitterly envious and resentful of the success his younger brother had made out of his adversity.

But how did Seth get himself transported as a

convict to New South Wales?

By now my attitude to Knottle was changing. Now I was hanging on his every word. Fortunately, though, I still kept my little recorder well placed, ready to capture the rest of the address.

"It appears from old letters that the Honourable Basil has fortunately preserved," said Knottle, "that the squire was aware of his younger brother, the Colonel, having an interest in the farmer's daughter. The squire disapproved of this. So," he said, leaning forward and looking directly into the audience for the first time, "according to the instruction he gave Amos Chevally by letter – of which letter the Honourable Basil unfortunately has no copy – Amos was to negotiate an appropriate payment to the farmer, in respect of the withdrawal of the horse from the meet. And, in return, if this negotiation was successful, the squire would order the farmer to make his daughter available for marriage to Amos. That was the bargain that apparently Amos agreed to."

"That's the sort of thing they did in those days." Muriel informed the gaping audience. "Isn't that so, Phineas."

To give Knottle his due, this was the first of Muriel's frequent interruptions that he chose to ignore. Continuing to look straight at the audience, he revealed the fact that I had already just realised.

"Although Amos did exactly as the squire required of him," he said, "the marriage with the farmer's daughter was never arranged and according to a story that is still preserved – and quoted – in the Summerfield family, she, Agnes, was said to have stated, I would rather die a thousand deaths than have to be married to Amos Chevally."

Perhaps I should have felt resentment at hearing this – after all, here was this girl not only rejecting the idea of marrying my great-grandfather, but giving a not-too-favourable opinion about him at the same time. But all I could think was, "Good on you, girl. Stay on the ball, get yourself out here to New South Wales, and become the great- grandmother of the girl I'm beginning to fall for."

Muriel, who had obviously expected some sort of reaction from the Amos descendants that she could take objection to, was looking disappointed when this hadn't happened.

"Go on, Phineas," she urged, "tell us what happened next."

Knottle cleared his throat. "To be perfectly honest," he said, "neither Miss Fotheringham nor the Honourable Basil was able to give me a reliable indication. So I have taken the liberty of proceeding on the basis of surmise."

What he meant by this obviously went over the heads of some of the listeners, and a surge of muttering had to be subdued by Muriel, after which Knottle continued.

"What I think happened," he said, "is that Seth

Chevally, deprived of the opportunity of demonstrating his superior horsemanship at the meet, and perhaps also of impressing the girl he admired, made a fateful decision. And that decision was, to surreptitiously take the farmer's horse out of the livery stables where he worked and take it to the meet anyway. And then, to enter the race from which the horse's owner, who it must be remembered was also the father of the girl he admired, had just been paid – or I would say, bribed – to withdraw the horse from."

At this point, Muriel rose in triumph and ordered us to thank Knottle for what she called his long-overdue illumination of the family history.

"Mr Knottle's informative lecture is now over," she informed us, "and before we disperse to enjoy the barbecue, we will thank him in the usual manner." She led a round of clapping before steering Knottle out of the room in the direction of Harry's barbecue and the tables we had helped to set up there.

But I wasn't satisfied. I turned off my recorder, replaced it in my pocket, and said to June, "I want to hear more from this bloke."

She smiled. "Let's catch up with him outside," she said.

CHAPTER 5

The family history suddenly gets more interesting

I don't know if you've ever been to a barbecue where they roast a whole sheep on a spit – I know I hadn't, so it was quite interesting to see how Harry was dealing with it. By the time June and I had got outside, he'd taken the carcass – now fully roasted – off the spit and was carving it up on a wooden tray on one of the tables.

It was a wonder to me that Muriel wasn't standing over him and giving directions, but I could see her over on the other side of the crowd, introducing Knottle to some of those newcomers she'd gathered up earlier for her tour of the homestead.

"Let's have something to eat," said June. "We can buttonhole him later, when Muriel's gone off to the kitchen to supervise the washing up."

So that's exactly what we did, and I have to say that the meal was a knockout – the mutton was tender and juicy and Harry's wife Merle had sent out from the kitchen two big trays of crisp looking baked potatoes and some jugs of gravy. June helped herself to one of the salads, which she said was all she wanted, and we found seats at the end of one of the trestle tables, on the other side of the gathering away from the area being dominated by Muriel.

"What is it that you want to find out from Mr Knottle?" June wanted to know.

"Well," I replied, between mouthfuls, "didn't you notice how Muriel cut him off just as he was getting to what happened after Seth was stopped from riding what would have been the winning horse?"

"Y-es," she said slowly, "I suppose that's really important, because it would explain how he came to be prosecuted and sent out here as a convict."

"Too right it would," I said, "and I bet Knottle knows all about it, and Muriel does too, but she wanted to play down the convict aspect of the story and that's why she wouldn't let him go any further with it."

"That's funny, isn't it," said June. "I've never had any problem admitting to having a convict in the family history. After all, if it hadn't been for what so many of them accomplished after they'd served their sentences,

69

we wouldn't have the country we live in today."

"Well," I said, "that's the difference between you and Muriel. Or one of them, at least."

In my mind I went over some of the other differences – between a bossy, self-opinionated snob and a sweet-natured and beautiful girl who was prepared to put up with me and keep me company – the comparison could go on and on, and fortunately I had the sense to keep it to myself and not say anything that might have disturbed the easy relationship that was developing between us.

Soon, as we finished our meal, we could see Muriel ordering people around her to stack their used plates and she hurried away in the direction of the kitchen.

"The coast is clear," June whispered conspiratorially, and I couldn't help grinning at the harmless joke we were sharing. "Let's go," I replied, and we made our way over to where Knottle, abandoned by Muriel, was finishing his meal.

"Mr Knottle," said June, "may we have a word with you?"

He gave us a look of vague surprise, and I remembered how he'd reacted when I laughed at him trying to saddle me with an Indian ancestor.

"I – I – yes, yes –" he stuttered, "is it about my research?"

"It is," I said, "and maybe we could find a quiet corner where I can ask you a couple of questions."

It was just then that one of Harry's kids appeared alongside of us, holding a tray with glasses and a bottle. "Home brew for anyone?" he asked.

"Oh – oh, no – no thanks," said Knottle, "not when I have to ride my bike to Willow Vale tonight."

"I think we'll give it a miss too," said June, and I could tell that she knew I wouldn't have cared much for a sample of the home brew, despite the fact that it was my great grandfather Amos who'd first produced it, in India.

"We can go back to the house," said June. "It'll be comfortable there, and no-one to disturb us."

As we walked back to the room we'd left earlier, I thought perhaps I should tell Knottle about my pocket reorder. There'd been a couple of guys at work who'd got into trouble for not declaring conversations that they'd recorded with clients.

I needn't have worried, however. "Oh!" said Knottle, "you found my lecture interesting enough to want a copy of it. That's – that's – really rather flattering, Mr Horsburgh."

"Just call me Roger," I said, and June chipped in, "I'm June."

With this chummy feeling established, we re-entered the now empty sitting room and June switched on the overhead light. And this time, I steered us towards the two-seater couch, where June and I sat together while Knottle pulled round one of the chairs to face us.

"There is more that I can tell you," he said. At this stage I thought I should show him my little recorder, which I did, and asked him if he minded if I turned it on.

Knottle looked really pleased and actually smiled. "Not at all, not at all," he replied. "I'm glad you find my investigations into the Chevally family interesting." So I switched on, and once again I can give you a word-for-word report of what he was able to add to what he'd said earlier.

"Before I begin," he said, "I must ask you to be discreet. There is information to add that Matron Chevally – er – Muriel – with whom, as you may know, I have – er – an understanding – would rather not make available to the wider family."

"Easy to see why not," I said, but June gave me a warning look and said, "Do go on, Mr Knottle."

"Yes, yes, yes" he said, "I will take up the story of Seth Chevally, at the point where his brother had been instrumental in preventing him from riding in the meet."

June and I settled down on the couch to listen, and our hands touched, sending a thrill through my whole body.

"Seth Chevally," Knottle began, "although young, was not devoid of spirit. And when he was informed by the owner of the livery stable that he would not be riding in the meet, he took matters into his own hands. On the pretext of taking the horse for its daily exercise, he rode it off to where the meet was being held, in the grounds of the Summerfield manor house, and lined up at the starting post with the other contestants."

I thought to myself, I'll bet that old squire, whoever he was, would have been furious when he saw that happening.

"As you might imagine," continued Knottle, "Seth easily won the race and was enthusiastically applauded by certain sectors of the crowd."

But not by rotten old Squire Summerfield, I thought.

"This was where events took an unfortunate turn," said Knottle, giving us an earnest look. "As Seth was preparing to leave the meet and ride the horse back to the livery stables, the livery stable owner, supported by the squire and accompanied by the local police constable, appeared on the scene, announcing to the public, 'That horse is stolen and the man in the saddle is the man who stole it'."

What a rotten act I thought – but just what you might expect from the so-called landed gentry.

"Seth was detained," Knottle explained, "and the squire, who had hereditary powers that today we would associate with a magistrate, pronounced him guilty of the theft of a horse and remanded him to appear before the local quarter sessions, where he was convicted and sentenced to seven years servitude in the penal colony of New South Wales."

"Despite his intention of returning the horse," said June. "His real offence was that he'd really only borrowed it without permission, not stolen it."

"What you might call today," I said, "a miscarriage of justice."

"I wonder how Amos felt," said June, "being responsible for making his young brother appear to be a criminal."

"Ah," said Knottle. "I have no evidence of how he felt, that is a territory into which the historian does not often like to trespass. But I do know what he did."

"Which was?" I prompted.

"I emphasise again," Knottle responded, "that I divulge this information on the understanding that you respect my request to keep it between yourselves."

I thought to myself, I've really underestimated this bloke. Whether he's on with Muriel or not, he knows the difference between what people want to think about something and what the evidence tells them they should think.

"Let me guess, " I said, in response to a feeling that was beginning to overwhelm me. "Amos had got himself so deeply into the deception that he couldn't see a way out of it."

"My conclusion exactly," said Knottle, rewarding me with a nod of approval.

"So, what did he do next?" I asked.

"It's a little complex," said Knottle, "and I assure you that without the assistance of the Honourable Basil Summerfield, I would not have obtained the lead I needed to further illuminate the situation."

My curiosity was really aroused. "So, what was this Basil bloke able to tell you?" I asked.

"It concerns the squire's younger brother, the Colonel," he replied.

"You mean that guy home on holidays from India who was trying to race off Agnes," I said.

Here followed a bit of conversation between the three of us, which I've left out, as I tried to explain what I'd meant by 'race off' – a term that they didn't seem familiar with in Melon Flats.

"It is certain," Knottle went on, "from copies of letters which I have had the privilege of being shown by the Honourable Basil, that Colonel Summerfield's domestic arrangements in Bengal did not include marriage."

"But you said –," I started to say, before June put her hand on my arm and said quietly, "Just hear Mr Knottle out, please Roger."

"To all intents and purposes," Knottle went on, "within the Indian context, Colonel Summerfield may be regarded as having a wife. She was the daughter of a local minor Indian aristocrat, whose territory the Colonel's regiment had successfully defended from an incursion by local brigands."

"Coo!" I exclaimed. "Well, at least the guy was good for something."

"So the Indian landowner must also have thought," said Knottle, "seeing that he gave permission for the cohabitation of his daughter with the Colonel."

"So it was really a marriage in terms of the local customs," said June, "but not in the eyes of the Church of England."

"Quite so, quite so," replied Knottle, "certain local religious ceremonies were observed, but the marriage was never registered with the British Army."

"So," I said, "it would probably be possible for that Colonel bloke to think that although he was married in India, back in England he wasn't."

"That may well have been the case," agreed Knottle, "although of course we have no evidence of the working of the Colonel's mind in these or indeed any other matters."

"Well," I said, "at least Agnes sent him off with a flea in his ear."

"Yes," said Knottle, "and of course, anyway, the Colonel was considerably older than Agnes. A whole generation, in fact."

"And she," put in June, "was already in love with Seth."

"So where did this leave Amos?" I asked.

"Well," said Knottle, "although Amos had carried

out the instructions of the squire, to the detriment of his young brother of course, the desired result had not been forthcoming. Being the man he was, Amos was not slow to voice his dissatisfaction and one of the letters shown to me is a request from Amos to the squire, asking for what he called a 'consideration'. What precisely Amos would have had in mind we don't know, but we do know how the squire responded."

"So Amos got something out of doing his brother in," I said. "Doesn't say much for him, I would have thought."

"What was it that the squire did for him?" asked June.

"That we know exactly," said Knottle. "The squire actually put in writing, to his brother the Colonel, the suggestion that Amos should accompany the Colonel back to Bengal where there was a prospect of conducting a lucrative liquor trade, which the Colonel could assist in setting up."

"And that's how Amos got to be in India!" I exclaimed.

"Exactly," said Knottle.

"I guess, after what he did to Seth, he wouldn't have been keen to stay around in England," I said. "And this liquor trade in India, was it selling grog to the British soldiers?"

"That appears to be what subsequent generations of the family have thought," said Knottle. "But the facts are otherwise."

"Crikey," I said. "Don't tell me Amos started selling grog to the Indians."

"No," said Knottle. "But it is essential to understand that at this point in the history of British India, there had developed a considerable community of what we refer to today as Anglo-Indians."

"Oh!" said June. "That would be, people of mixed blood – half Indian and half English. Probably the children of some of the English soldiers stationed there."

"And not only the day-to-day soldiers," Knottle continued. "Don't forget that Colonel Summerfield also had an Indian wife."

"And children, too, I expect," I said.

"Just so," said Knottle. "And in fact, we know that the Colonel had two daughters by his Indian wife. Because of their father's position, they were the social leaders of the local Anglo-Indian community."

"Did they have the Summerfield name?" asked June.

"They did," Knottle replied. "Their names were Myra and Nina Summerfield."

"Aren't we getting a bit off the track?" I said, "Interesting as it is, I don't see what all this has got to do with the Chevally family – of which I appear to be a part, even though my name's Horsburgh," I added, giving June a look.

"It might prove to be more important than you think," said Knottle, "if I tell you that after eighteen months in Bengal, Amos Chevally was married, by the British Army Chaplain, to the elder daughter of Colonel Summerfield – Miss Myra Summerfield."

Well, I have to say, this floored me completely. "You mean to say," I gasped, "that one of my ancestors was that bastard, with a wife and family in India, who came home and tried to seduce Agnes? June's great-grandmother?" To say it out loud like that was appalling and I couldn't help thinking, what's June going to think of me now.

But when I looked at June, I could see that she hadn't taken it to heart as I had done. Instead, with a smile, she said to Knottle, "so Roger and I do have an Indian ancestor – some Indian landowner I think you called him?"

"Yes, I've been able to fully authenticate the connection," he replied. "The ancient Indian aristocratic system is incredibly complicated but the great-great-great grandfather that you two share with each other was undoubtedly of that caste and standing."

And that is when the full realisation of what Knottle had just told us burst upon me. "You mean," I said, "that when Amos came up here to Murrendebri and opened his first version of what is now June's Royal Hotel, his wife – my great-grandmother – what did you call her – Myra – came here too?"

"That's an aspect that I haven't investigated," he replied, "but from all accounts, she remained in Sydney with her two small children, Robert and Margery Chevally, until Amos managed to have his Royal Empire Hotel constructed, a notable achievement in the pioneering village of Murrendebri."

"The first stone building in the village," said June.

"And two-storied, like Seth's homestead − so as not to be outdone by his young brother, who he never spoke to," I added.

A profound silence seemed to descend over us and it was at this point that I switched off my recorder. I was busy with thoughts of how Amos might have felt, arriving from India − with his young family, including my grandmother Margery − whose name I was only now hearing for the first time − coming up here from where he'd landed in Sydney and finding Agnes not only happily married to Seth but mistress of a fine new house. A veritable mansion by the colonial standards of the time. And I wondered how Seth would have felt too, having the brother who had betrayed him turn up, probably unexpectedly, in the situation here that he must have worked very hard to create for himself in the land to which he had been deported, however unjustly, as a criminal.

It was June who broke the silence.

"Mr Knottle," she said, "I would like to thank you, and I know that I speak on behalf of Roger too, for letting us into a part of our family story that has until now remained hidden from both of us."

This startled me out of my reverie and I added my thanks to what June had just said.

"Well," said Knottle, "I'm only glad that I've been able to be of assistance. I'm afraid that not all members of your family have accepted the news as eagerly as you have."

"You mean Muriel, I think," said June quietly.

"Er – well – yes," was Knottle's response. He looked down at the floor in a shamefaced sort of way and for the first time I actually felt sorry for him, but at the same time, a strange sort of joy went through me as I finally recognised and understood the fact that the relationship I'd had with Fiona back in Sydney was permanently finished – and furthermore, that I had no regrets about that at all.

As the three of us sat there, immersed in our thoughts, the door was suddenly flung open and Muriel appeared.

"Why, Phineas!" she exclaimed. "Here you are. I've been looking everywhere for you. What are you doing with these two?"

No doubt about it, June knows how to handle a difficult situation.

"We wanted to compliment Mr Knottle," she said, with a warm smile in Knottle's direction, "for his excellent address, which this evening has filled in so much of our family history for us, and I am sure has also repaid him for all the hard work he had to do in Staffordshire in order to discover it."

Knottle smiled gratefully and said "Thank you," and then, as if Muriel had already issued one of her unspoken instructions, said hesitantly, "Yes, it must almost be time to be making tracks."

"It certainly is," said Muriel. "Now. Can you remember what you've done with your motor bike?"

"Oh dear," he said, "I remember that I rode it down here this morning…"

"Well of course you did, you silly man," said Muriel archly. "But where did you park it?"

"Ah!" said Knottle. "I remember now. It's under that big tree near the church."

"Good!" said Muriel. "You can ride out in front of me so that I can keep an eye on you when we get on the main road."

Then, turning to us, she said, "Everyone's leaving now, we've got the kitchen tidied up and all the people who stayed to help have put the tables away." No doubt the heavy emphasis she put on 'stayed to help' was intended to make June and me feel guilty but I didn't feel inclined to point out to Muriel that it was us who had helped to put the tables out earlier.

"It's been a great day," I heard myself saying, and June added, "thanks to your organisation, Muriel."

"Oh well," said Muriel, "I'm always pleased to

remember the achievements of my great-grandfather Seth. Now come along Phineas, I have to get back to Willow Vale to check on the nurse I've left in charge."

With that, and with Knottle in tow, Muriel left the room, leaving June and me together on the couch. But we weren't there long.

"Come on," said June, "we must thank Harry and the family before we leave." She rose, and I did too and followed her out into the hall and along to the courtyard. There, Harry and all his family were enjoying a well-earned tuck-in to what was left of the roasted sheep and the salads.

We said our thanks and good-byes and set out along the homestead's gravel drive down towards the creek. The sun was almost setting and there was a faint glow in the west but it was still possible to see the way. I just didn't want this day to end. I had to say something.

"June," I said, as we walked along, "I've got to tell you. This is the best day out I've had in years. And…" That's as far as I got.

I couldn't think of how to say it. I wanted to tell her that it was because of being with her. But the words wouldn't come. I could have kicked myself.

June didn't seem to notice my difficulty. "Wasn't it, though!" she exclaimed. "I never expected to get such a full explanation of the relationship between Seth and Amos. We really have a lot to thank Mr Knottle for."

Well, I couldn't disagree with that. But I was still

agonising over what could I say next.

Soon we were crossing the little footbridge and approaching our parked cars. This was when June turned to me and said, "well – Roger – the day's over. It's been great meeting you – I hope you'll sleep well tonight, and I'll see you in the morning, before you leave."

She paused for a moment, and then continued, "Now that you've established a family connection, if you're ever up this way again, perhaps we could meet again – that's if you –"

Something in the way that June said this released in me what I had been wanting to say to her. I seized the opportunity.

"June," I said, "meeting you has meant more to me than – than I can say." I could feel the words tumbling out of me, as though I had no control over what I was saying and yet I didn't want to stop.

"What I'd just like to say," I said, "that forgetting about all the family details, I don't often meet – that is – what I mean is..." and here, I'm afraid, I stumbled into incoherence.

June laughed at this – but it wasn't the sort of laugh that Fiona used to give me when I tried to explain my feelings to her. No, this was a laugh that seemed to say, I understand, and there's no need to go on, this is something that you and I can agree on. And, in that way that she has, June took over the conversation and made sense of it.

"Roger," she said, "I think that after meeting today, you and I might become good friends. Quite regardless of being related. That's, of course, if you –"

"That's exactly how I feel!" I burst out. "Why can't we see each other again – sometime."

"I think I could look forward to that," June replied, in that remote tone of voice I'd noticed before, as if she wasn't really interested in what we were talking about. But the look on her face told a different story.

I drove back to Murrendebri in what I can only describe now as a confusion of rosy feelings. It had been only just over twenty-four hours that I had met June, and yet I felt that I'd known her for ages. But what astounded me was how different I felt about everything. The world seemed to open up a new vista – a bit like a rose blossom unfurling its petals and showing a beauty that you hadn't known was there.

I pulled up in front of the Royal, realising that I had no idea where June's accommodation was. Not that I was thinking of trying to see her at this hour, we'd already said goodbye back at Melon Flats – but just to know where she was, that was all I wanted.

The hotel bar seemed to be doing good business, judging by the raucous sounds I could hear coming out of it as I walked along the corridor to the staircase. Usually, after a day out somewhere, I'd be tempted to go and have a few beers before bed, but tonight I felt different. I didn't want company, I wanted dreams. I know that might sound stupid, but it's the only way I can put it in a way that makes sense to me.

The stairs were in darkness but it was easy enough to judge where I was going and I pulled my door key out of my pocket ready to unlock my room. And that's when a very peculiar thing happened. The key wouldn't work and the door remained stubbornly locked.

I tried to work out what was wrong. No, I thought, I haven't got a different key, this is the one that June handed to me when I registered. Maybe there was something wrong with the door? But what could have happened, to make the key inoperable? I peered at the door – and as I did so, I noticed the number on it. My room was No.2. What I had been trying to do, was to unlock the door of No.1.

Stupid mistake, wasn't it. But I couldn't explain to myself why I had walked past No.2 and tried to open the room next to it, No.1. Nor could I explain to myself why I had the feeling that No.1 was the room that I should be sleeping in.

I remembered then the odd feeling I'd had yesterday, when June had shown me into No.2. The feeling that it wasn't the room that I'd expected it to be. I quickly put all these useless thoughts out of my mind, went back to the door of No.2 and unlocked it, switched on the light, and stood for a moment in the doorway wondering if I was going to have a repeat of yesterday's reaction. Nothing happened. Of course it didn't, I told myself, it's all imagination. Yesterday I'd called it travel fatigue – tonight it must be the overwhelming pleasure of becoming part of this strange and curious family that

I had found myself suddenly belonging to.

When I'd been to the bathroom and got ready for bed, I carefully locked the door. I didn't want any more peculiar sensations, I wanted to think over and re-experience what I already knew was going to be one of the most significant days of my life.

Although sleep came easily, it wasn't an easy sleep. I know I must have had a lot running through my consciousness because early the next morning I woke up to escape from a nightmare I was having. I only remember the bit of it that was happening as I woke up but that was enough to jolt me wide awake. I was on the deck of a ship – a sailing ship, by the look of it – and the sea was raging around the vessel and threatening to roll right over it. I wanted to escape but I was weighed down by all the stuff I had to carry – things that looked like wooden barrels – that if the sea swept them away I would be left with nothing. It was the anxiety of this impossible situation that woke me – and it took me a moment to actually realise that I wasn't at sea, I was in a comfortable bed in the Royal Hotel, Murrendebri, having just spent the day before with the girl I'd been looking for in my dream.

It didn't take me long to get up and get ready to leave. I felt a bit desolate as I walked down the stairs and headed for the breakfast room. I should have made some arrangement, I told myself, to see June again this morning before I set out for Sydney. So, imagine my surprise to see her standing at the doorway of the breakfast room, smiling at me and wishing me a good morning.

"We're short staffed," she explained. "So I'm standing in until our relief girl gets here. She lives up in Willow Vale so I didn't expect her to get here before we had to start breakfast. Would you like bacon and eggs? You seemed to enjoy that yesterday."

"I'd love that," I said.

"Coming up," said June, and she turned towards the kitchen.

"And maybe if we could…" I tried to add. But June had already disappeared and all I could do was wait to see if she would return.

CHAPTER 6

I think about my life and decide to make some improvements

You know when you're in a restaurant say, and maybe eating there on your own, as I frequently have to do? You finish your meal but you're not in a hurry to get up and go about your business? Then the table staff start hovering, and after awhile they might start asking you if you want anything else – even though it's obvious that you don't?

Well, that's what it was like at the Royal Hotel, that morning after the day out at Melon Flats. I just couldn't delay my departure any longer and with no sign of June anywhere, I just got up, picked up my bag that I'd brought downstairs with me, and went out to the office to pay my bill.

With June still somewhere in the kitchen area, as I imagined coping with her staff shortage, I was half expecting the office to be unmanned, but behind the desk there was a guy I hadn't seen before. Judging by the clothes he had on, he might have been the gardener, or maybe the hotel handyman.

"Mr Horsburgh?" he said, as I came in. "Miss Chevally's left a message for you," and he handed me a note. Despite the fact that June must have written it in a hurry, the writing was neat and clear and I can still remember what it said.

"Roger – I hope you've enjoyed your stay. Don't forget us, maybe come again sometime. Make sure Wayne gives you a 10% family discount. Travel safely, June."

As I settled the bill, I said to the guy Wayne, "I'll pay the full amount, please."

He looked doubtful and said, "Miss Chevally told me –"

"Just do it," I said, "and give June – Miss Chevally – my best wishes."

"Ok," he said – and that was that.

As I walked to my car, parked on the street just in front, I looked back at the hotel and thought, "My great-grandfather built this place." It gave me a very curious feeling to think this – sort of half-nostalgia and half-frustration, I can't think of any other way to describe it. It was as though there was something there that I'd left undone. Which was true – I hadn't managed to say goodbye to June as I had wanted to.

The drive back to Sydney was full of self-recriminations. As I thought over the brief and startlingly enjoyable day I'd had in June's company, I kept punishing myself, thinking why didn't I do this, why hadn't I said that. I hadn't even thought to get June's phone number. Still, I guessed, I could always contact her through the number of the hotel reception. But would she want to hear from me? I know she'd said we could become friends and as her note said, maybe I could come to Murrendebri another time – but was this enough?

It wasn't until I got back to my house in Balmain, and noticed that there were messages on my landline voicemail, that I cleared my mind and prepared to deal with those. The first message was from Fiona.

"Darling!" the recording screamed, "why haven't you rung me? Waiting for your call – don't leave it too long!"

What was I supposed to make of this, I wondered.

The second message was even more specific. "Darling," said Fiona's voice in that wheedling tone I'd come to recognise that she used, whenever she wanted to get me to do something that she wanted me to do, "ring me immediately you get this. I've got some important news."

I've already said that I knew that Fiona and I were finally finished – I recognised that during the day I spent with June at Melon Flats. But what could Fiona possibly mean when she said she had 'important news'? Although I knew, from previous experience, that she specialised in shock revelations which often turned out to be entirely pointless, habit intervened and I dialed her number.

"Darling!" she greeted me. "I knew you'd call."

I thought to myself, did you now. But although I'd decided to stay calm and remote, old habits die hard and before I knew what I was saying, I'd asked her to tell me what was this important news she was so keen to inform me about.

"Darling," she said, lowering her voice a register or two, "the most awful thing has happened."

"Don't tell me you're pregnant," I said.

"Don't be ridiculous darling," she snapped. "You know very well that we —"

"I was joking," I said. "Come on. What is this awful news you're so keen to tell me?"

"Darling – it's about my dear little flat, where you and I have been so happy together."

Well, I thought, that statement needs a bit of a qualification. Especially now, after the surprise I'd had in the way I'd unexpectedly enjoyed my Melon Flats weekend.

"Go on," I said.

"Well – my flat's been sold. Sold from under me, and I've been given a week to move out."

"Bad luck," I said.

"So," Fiona continued without waiting for any further comment, "what I thought was, why not move in with you, and we can see each other every day, just as we've always wanted, and your house has such a lovely view over the water —"

"Hang on, hang on, hang on," I said. "I seem to remember that you wanted to call off our relationship. No sleeping together, those were your instructions if I remember correctly. What would you do if you moved in here, sleep on the floor?"

"Oh darling," she exclaimed, "of course I didn't mean that to be a permanent arrangement. Just a little break from the ordinary, you know —"

Something flashed through my head and at last I knew I had something to put into words in an answer to Fiona, and I didn't even have to count to six. I knew exactly what I wanted to say, and I said it.

"Fiona," I said, "you've buggered me about for six months or more. If I'm so 'ordinary' like you've just said, why didn't you call it off six months ago when you realised that I'm what you've called 'ordinary'? What's so ordinary about me anyway?"

I was getting quite heated, and plunged right on.

"And now, apart from that," I continued, "you've got the nerve to suggest coming over here and living with me, because you've got tossed out of your flat and you have to find somewhere else to live. Don't you have somebody else you can impose yourself on?"

"Well!" said Fiona. "What a nasty, spiteful person you are. I'm not entirely without friends, you know, in fact now that I come to think of it, Adrian has said that he'd welcome it if I wanted to stay at his place. He has a lovely house in Darlinghurst, so close to the city —"

"What!" I exploded. I couldn't help myself. "Who is this Adrian bloke? How long have you and him been on visiting terms? Would that have anything to do with deciding not to sleep with me? Except now, when you need alternative accommodation —"

And now, the illumination finally dawned. "This Adrian," I said. "You've been sleeping with him, haven't you."

There was a sharp intake of breath on the other end of the line.

Then silence.

"Maybe you haven't had time to find out how 'ordinary' he is yet?" I prompted. "But don't worry, I'm sure you'll get round to it."

"Well," said Fiona, in her nastiest tone, "if that is your attitude then it's goodbye. I never want to see you or hear from you again."

"That suits me just fine," I said, and hung up.

It's not often that I need a reviver, but after the long drive and then that altercation over the phone with Fiona, what I needed was a scotch and a good long think, so I poured myself a double measure and sat down to review my life.

Like I've said, a family identity was never very important to me. Although my parents seemed to remain on good terms with each other, they got divorced while I was still at school, in Year 10 if I remember, and for awhile I wasn't sure which one of them was going to be a permanent sort of parent – and as it turned out, neither of them appeared to want to take on that sort of responsibility for me. They were both busy, I suppose, creating new lives for themselves. My mother ended up falling for some guy from New Zealand and moved over there to be with him, which left me alone in the house with my father because she took my sister with her. Not that this was bad, but Dad and I didn't exactly hit it off and never had very much to say to each other. Besides, Dad was – or I should say, is – an obsessive sort of guy whose main interest in life seems to be his work at the Main Roads Board where, to give him his due, he seems to have been very successful. My sister Anne didn't come back until she got married to that dag she hooked up with so as a result I really hardly know her and neither of us seem to make much of an effort to keep in touch with each other.

It was purely by chance that I got into the insurance business. I did one of those work experience stints while I was still at school, in a real insurance office where for some reason the manager noticed that I had what he called 'potential'. He told me that if I wanted to apply for a job there when I left school, he'd give it what he called 'favourable consideration'.

Well, as there wasn't anything else on the horizon when I left school that's what I did and I'd worked for the same company ever since.

As I was thinking about all this, that was when the idea occurred to me that maybe the company was really like a sort of family. Or maybe that's how I've come to think of it, as a kind of substitution for the real family I didn't have. Or that I couldn't even imagine having, until last weekend, when a whole new vista of what a family means opened up before me, up at Melon Flats.

Sitting on the divan and looking out over the moonlight glistening on the water of the Harbour, I was starting to feel a bit mellow by this point – I enjoy a drop of single malt occasionally, and the one I happened to have open on this occasion was a particularly good one. I relaxed and thought of June.

Although I didn't realise it just then, a new feeling was coming over me. I know now that it was the inclination to want a relationship that I could rely on as a permanent one. Meaning, that something was taking me beyond the search for company and mere physical pleasure. I know now that I was moving towards something I'd never yet discovered or experienced – real love. Yes, as I sat there, I realised that this new experience was what I wanted. And I wondered whether, if I played my cards right, how I might be able to achieve it.

But then the doubts set in. Did I have any of the winning cards in my hand that I would need. What would it take, to demonstrate to June that for me, she was everything I would ever want? Because that's how I felt about her. After knowing her for just one day. And was this enough time to be as certain as I was about this feeling? What sort of tests would I have to face, to prove not only to June but to myself, that these feelings were really and unassailably genuine? And now the inevitable self-assessment set in.

Yes, I was physically healthy. Although not a sports addict, I'd managed to keep in good physical shape. Mentally, although I know I'm not the sharpest knife in the drawer, I'm pretty good at my job, with what I'd call good prospects. But there was something else that I felt I needed to consider, and I cast my mind about trying to identify what it was.

I suppose you could say that I was getting philosophical, as I sat there looking at the Harbour and taking an occasional sip of scotch. Yes, I had a body, that was obvious. Yes, I had a mind, that was obvious too. But somehow I was coming to the realisation, these weren't the sum total of what made me a human being. There was another element, wasn't there. Call it heart, call it soul, call it whatever some of those religious gurus call it – there is an element of us all that is more than just body and mind. And, as I sat there, it dawned on me in a shattering sort of realisation, that whatever this third element was, it was the one that I needed to guide me towards a fulfilling life, and that, I knew now, needed to include my relationship with June.

Even though I was full of doubts I felt strangely elated, and it wasn't just the scotch that was doing that. The whole world seemed to have taken on a sort of glow that it hadn't had before. That's what it seemed like, and I was certain that it had happened to me because of how I felt about June, I was certain of that. I asked myself, can I really fall in love as quickly as this? – but the only reply was, Yes; I can; and I have.

That night, I had a long, dreamless sleep and woke in the morning remembering that it was Monday, a working day. I enjoy my work but that day I felt that I had other things to think about.

At the company I had got along pretty well with the guy who was then in charge of the claims division. It suddenly occurred to me that he'd told me I had an accumulation of leave owing to me and that he wanted me to take it, or at least some of it, before it accumulated more. I rang him up straight away.

"You've got nearly six weeks owing to you," he informed me. "Take as much of it as you want – right now. All of it, if you want to."

I settled for two whole weeks, starting today, and then sat down with a fresh cup of coffee to try to decide what to do next. The decision was obvious. I dialled the number of the Murrendebri Royal Hotel.

As the phone was ringing, I was trying to imagine what I'd say to whoever answered. I hoped it wouldn't be Wayne, the guy I'd paid my bill with. It wasn't.

"Royal Hotel," said June's voice.

"Oh!" I said, "Hello June. Er – it's –"

"It's Roger!" she replied. "How are you? Did you

get back to Sydney all right?"

"Yes," I said. "I'm just ringing because – because –"

"Did you leave something behind?" asked June.

Through my mind flashed the sort of thing you see on all those soap operas on TV – where the guy would come out with something like 'Yes – what I've left behind is my heart – and it's in your hands,' or some crap like that.

I certainly didn't intend going down that track.

"No," I said, "I didn't leave anything behind. Just that – well – I've got some unexpected leave from work, and I wondered – if I happen to be up your way again –"

"Oh!" said June. "Would you like to call in? That would be nice." She paused for a moment. "Why don't you come up next weekend, if you can? The local Jockey Club will be running the annual Murrendebri Cup meeting on Saturday. You could stay here, at the hotel – if you like, we could have the day out together."

June had made it so easy – I just gasped. "That would be just great," I managed to say. "Hey! Are there any restaurants up there that I could take you out to? Give you a break from the hotel?"

June laughed at that. "Not here," she said, "but up at Willow Vale they've got what I'm told is a good new Indian restaurant. Perhaps, as we appear to share an Indian great-great-great grandfather, it might be interesting to see what it's like."

"Sounds good to me," I said. "Did somebody recommend it?" I didn't want to take June to some crummy joint, like that last outing I'd had with Fiona.

June laughed again. "Well, actually," she said, "it was Muriel who told me about it. She lives up there, you know."

"And she's been to it?" I asked. I wasn't inclined to trust Muriel's opinion about anything.

"Oh no!" said June. "I think she only insisted on telling me about it to emphasise the fact that, being descended from Seth and Agnes, she hasn't any Indian ancestor – unlike you and me, and the rest of the Amos descendants."

"Well," I said, "that also lets her out of being related to that Summerfield mob that her pal Mr Knottle was so keen on. Though I don't regard as being descended from Colonel Blimp, as we apparently are, as anything to be particularly proud of."

"No," June agreed, "and anyway, it's so far in the past that it's hardly relevant today."

"Instead," I said, "let's look forward to a day at the races." I wanted to add, 'together'; but I didn't want to press my luck in case that would sound too forward. "Is it ok if I arrive about the same time as before?"

"You'll find me in the office, as usual," June laughed.

"So," I said, "goodbye till next Friday afternoon!" and we both hung up.

I was so pleased with the way everything had turned out that I made myself another cup of coffee and went out and sat on the balcony. Then, it occurred to me – I'd agreed on a week's leave from work, and I wouldn't be going to Murrendebri till Friday. That left today and three other days with nothing to do!

I've never cared very much about how I look, but now that I had what was in effect a first date arranged with June, I wondered whether I shouldn't try to smarten up my appearance for the occasion. After all, she'd said we were going to the local Jockey Club meeting where there would be all sorts of locals. I didn't want June to feel embarrassed if I didn't match up with the local standards – whatever they might turn out to be. Definitely a haircut was called for as I hadn't had one for weeks.

That took care of most of the day, as I don't have a regular barber and I went up to the main street where there are several, to look them over. After I'd found one I liked the look of, I went in and had my usual 'short back and sides'. Then, on the way back, I passed this men's outfitter and to cut a long story short, after a lengthy investigation I invested in a new tweed sports jacket that I thought should be the sort of thing to wear to a country race meeting.

I spent Tuesday and Wednesday putting the house in order, just in case June should ever want to visit; not that I expected her to, as she lived up there in Murrendebri – but somehow, I felt that I needed to make it as clean and tidy as possible in order to match the feelings that the thought of her stirred up in me. And on Thursday, I gave the car a thorough clean, inside and out, ready for the excursion.

Friday dawned bright and sunny and I couldn't wait to get away. It's funny, but I've done a lot of travelling as part of work commitments and I've never taken all that much interest in the countryside that I pass through. Today, however, I seemed to notice everything. As I got further out of the city I could see people working in the paddocks, lots of animals feeding on the grass, and here and there a weatherboard farmhouse and outbuildings. All of this fed my anticipation of arrival in Murrendebri, where I was impatient to meet June again.

As I got nearer to the end of the trip I could recognise the places I'd seen on my first visit – the small creeks, the church with its square tower, the farmhouses with washing drying on the clotheslines. And soon, in front of me, was the Royal Hotel, with its faded sign and its uneven iron lace all along the balcony. I parked the car, jumped out and raced up the stone steps into the corridor, to be greeted by June standing at the door of the office.

"Welcome back!" she smiled, and without saying anything all I could do was to give her a big hug. It was only then that I found my voice.

"I've looked forward to coming here again so much," I said, with an unexpected burst of feeling. "Last weekend was a blast I'll never forget."

"I'm glad you feel like that," June said quietly. "I

enjoyed it too. Now, if you'd like to come along to the lounge, you might be ready for some refreshment after the drive from Sydney."

This time, June sat down with me on one of the lounges and took the cloth off a plate of cocktail snacks that was waiting on the nearby coffee table. "Help yourself," she said. "Would you like to have a beer? Fosters, wasn't it?"

I was really surprised to find myself refusing. I just didn't want anything else, but just to sit here, close to June, and enjoy the feeling of being with her again.

To be honest, I can't remember what we started talking about, but after awhile I asked June about the race meeting that we would be going to the next day.

"It's funny, isn't it," she said, "that so much of what we are today came from that other race meeting back in Staffordshire – the one that my ancestor, Seth, insisted on riding in – on an illegally borrowed horse that landed him here in Australia."

It was a sobering moment. "And that my ancestor, Amos, dobbed him in for," I said. "All because they both fancied the same girl."

"Well, you know the old saying," said June, "jealousy is a curse."

"It makes you wonder," I said, "why Amos would want to come to Australia. He must have been doing all right in India. Especially married to an Indian girl."

"Anglo-Indian," June corrected me. "I do know

something about great-grandmother Myra – though I didn't know that her father was Colonel Summerfield, which, as you remember, we learned from Mr Knottle last week."

"Yes, I hadn't forgotten." I said. "I don't suppose she would have been too keen to leave India and come to a place like this, without knowing anything about it."

"I'm not sure about that," said June. "In fact, I'm inclined to think that she might have encouraged Amos to make the move."

This was a surprising thought. "What on earth makes you think that?" I asked.

"Well," she said, "that chat that you and I had with Mr Knottle really set me thinking, and I remembered that there were some old files stacked at the back of a cupboard in the office that date from the early days of what Amos called the Royal Empire Hotel. So I got them out when I had a couple of hours to spare during the week, and made a quite surprising discovery."

"What was it?" I asked.

"Our great-grandmother Myra's diary," said June. "It's not in very good condition – the binding has given way and there seem to be some pages missing. But what there is of it makes interesting reading."

This seemed to strike a real chord in me and I felt a sort of thrill. "My great-grandmother's diary!" I exclaimed.

"Don't forget," June added, "that she's my great-grandmother too."

"I'm not too sure how that works," I said

"Simple," said June. "One of her daughters married Seth's son Robert, my grandfather. A marriage of first cousins – it often happened back then."

This was when I gave up trying to follow. All that mattered to me was that June and I had a connection, and if she was happy about it, so was I.

"So, tell me about this diary," I said.

"Well," said June, although it's called a diary on the cover, it seems to be more like an appointment book. There are lots of entries on certain dates about the things Myra and her sister Nina went to – including archery practice. They belonged to an archery club that had been set up in their community. Apparently it was an activity that the Anglo-Indians thought of as being typically English."

"Ah! So that's how archery came to Melon Flats," I said. "At least that mystery's solved. It was a sport that came with Myra, Amos's wife."

"Yes, and she was quite good at it, apparently," said June. "There are entries in her book about competitions with other archery clubs, and often notes about how her team performed."

"Nothing else?" I asked.

"Well," said June, "that's the thing. There are some occasional personal statements, and there's one in particular that I've made a copy of to show you," and she handed me a piece of paper. It was in her own neat handwriting, but the words were originally written by a mysterious great-grandmother I'd known nothing about until last week, but about whom I was now interested to find out more.

This was the entry that June showed me.

'Daddy is so cruel. Nina and I, both separately and together, have begged him to take us with him when he goes Home on furlough next month. But he won't. He says that we would be out of place in England. How can this be? When I tried to ask him to explain, all he said was that Nina and I are hybrids. That word I had to look up in our English Dictionary. It is a horrid word.'

"Hmmm," I said, after reading this. "Sounds like Myra – I can't call her great-grandmother – sounds like Myra's got Daddy's number all right."

I thought for a minute before I went on. "He was the bastard – sorry, June, I can't call him anything else – who spent his leave from India pursuing your great-grandmother, Agnes, a young girl half his age. From what Knottle told us, even his own brother disapproved of him."

"Sounds like a pattern," June said. "Brothers disagreeing."

"You mean Seth and Amos," I said. "Yeah – not good."

June gave me that smile of hers. "Let's not worry

about it today," she said. "And thanks for agreeing to come to the races tomorrow. I wasn't looking forward to going on my own."

"Well," I said, "like so much that seems to happen around here, it'll be a new experience for me. I've never been to a race meeting."

"There's a first time for everything," she replied, and suddenly looked away as she said it. I couldn't help wondering – was that a slight blush showing on her face? Maybe I imagined it.

"Considering that you're still part of the family reunion," she said, "I've given you room Number 1. We don't usually allocate it as a guest room, because when the hotel was built, Amos reserved it for himself as private quarters."

When I heard this, I can't describe the feeling that went through me. I must have looked a bit peculiar, because June asked me if I was feeling ok.

"Sure," I said, "probably just a bit weary after the trip." But I knew it wasn't that, and I remembered the strange encounter I'd had with the door of No.1 on my previous overnight at the hotel. I tried to shake off the feeling but it was difficult to dislodge.

I don't know what made me say it, but suddenly I was asking June if anyone had ever asked her if the place was haunted. She looked at me in surprise.

"No-o," she said slowly. Then she added, "but if you'd rather have No.2 again –"

"No! No!" I said. Then I tried to laugh it off. "Just give me the key, and I'll let you know in the morning if it's haunted or not."

"Nothing more to eat, before you turn in?" she asked.

"If your breakfast is as good tomorrow as it was last time, that's all I'll be dreaming about," I said.

"Goodnight then, and sleep well," she said, handing me the key. I started off, up the stairs.

CHAPTER 7

More about Myra ~ and a day out at the Picnic Races

I didn't feel anything unusual until I got to the top of the stairs, where again there was that feeling of a wall of darkness in front of me. As I stood there, waiting for my eyes to adjust, so that I could see my way through the dimness to the door of No.1, some words that I'd heard before somehow flashed through my head – only, this time, somewhere, somehow, it seemed as though I heard them spoken.

It was as though a voice, it was neither male nor female, was whispering inside my brain. This is what it said.

"The juice of the pomegranate lightens the heart for love."

As clear as a bell. And the funny thing was, I didn't find this at all unsettling, as it had been the first time I'd heard it somewhere in my head.

I reached the door, inserted my key, entered No.1 and switched on the light. The room was bigger than No.2 and the furnishings were similar, except that the bed, as I'd expected, was placed across the corner, not against the wall.

Also, there was a door in one of the side walls. I walked across and opened it. It gave into a large, old-fashioned bathroom. "Of course," I thought, this would have been Amos and Myra's private quarters. The bath was one of those big, cast iron ones lined with white enamel that bathrooms used to have in the old days. It was in perfect condition and I wondered if the tap marked 'H' would actually produce hot water, so I turned it on to find out.

Soon the stream of cold water turned warm, and then hot. "I'm going to have a bath!" I thought, put the bath plug in and with the help of the other tap marked 'C' adjusted the heat of the water.

I stripped off and got in.

Lying there, comfortably relaxed in the warm water, I began to think of my newly-discovered great-grandparents, Amos and Myra, who had lived here. How could they possibly have been happy together, I wondered. I already had my views about Amos, and his duplicity towards his young brother. But Myra – had she wanted to marry Amos, or was this another one of 'Daddy's' decisions that she had been made to accept?

I thought of that entry from her diary that June had shown me downstairs. Maybe there would be other bits of her writing that might throw some light on the situation Myra was in and how she felt about it. An Anglo-Indian daughter of an English colonel stationed in India; a father who had, in effect, refused to acknowledge her as his daughter.

I got out of the bath, let the water out and began to towel myself dry. Tomorrow, June and I were due to go to the races. But before we left the hotel, I decided, I would talk about these thoughts with June and see if we might have a look together at the diary Myra had left. Damaged and incomplete as it might be, there must be more clues in it about Myra's situation and how she felt about the life that fate had somehow designed for her to lead.

I wondered whether I'd have trouble getting to sleep in No. 1 but I needn't have worried – as soon as my head touched the pillow I must have gone straight off, for the next thing I knew was a shaft of the morning sun touching my face and I woke up refreshed and ready for whatever the day was to offer. And that, I hoped, meant breakfast with June.

As before, she was on duty at the dining room door, welcoming guests. She asked how I'd slept, and I said, "great". Then I asked if, after breakfast, I could have a look at what I was beginning to think of as Myra's diary.

"Sure," she replied. "We don't have to be in a hurry to get to the races. They won't run the Murrendebri Cup till this afternoon, 3 o'clock. When you've had breakfast, come to the office and we'll have a look at it together."

This was just what I'd hoped for, and when I got to the office I found that June had laid out the diary, in its various pieces, on a small side-table ready for our inspection.

"I've tried to keep the pages in sequence," she explained, "but there are several gaps – almost as though someone has removed some whole entries."

"Makes you wonder, doesn't it," I said. "Do you think that Myra might have done that herself?"

"Either that," she said, "or someone close to her who didn't like what she had to say; or, rather, what she had written about."

Neither June nor I said 'Amos' aloud but as we looked at each other it was clear to both of us that we both thought the same thing.

"Well, let's start here," said June, and she held up one of the pages. "She's crossed out the date," she said, "so perhaps it comes from an early section where there weren't any engagements noted."

I whipped out my mobile phone and took a picture of the page, before I'd read it, and I'm reproducing what it said here.

'Daddy arrived from his visit Home two days ago and this morning he called Nina and me into his office and

told us that he has brought a young Englishman with him who, he told us, would be suitable enough for one of us to marry. Although he did not say so in words, it was clear that one of us will have to decide to accept this man. After he had dismissed us, poor Nina collapsed in tears, she already has feelings for Daddy's adjutant, who seems to return her regard. All I can do is pray that this Englishman is someone who perhaps I can learn to love, as a wife should.'

After I'd read this, I turned to June. "This must have been written eighteen months before the marriage," I said. "Did you find anything else about whether a real relationship developed?"

I was feeling a great deal of sympathy for Myra, what a position that father of hers had put her in.

"She hasn't written anything about her first meeting with Amos," said June, "or if she has, it's been removed by whoever tore out some of the pages."

I didn't express my feelings to June but I was beginning to feel more than just annoyed. If Amos had fiddled with Myra's diary as we both seemed to think, it amounted to the kind of deception I knew only too well from people trying to put in dishonest insurance claims.

"Fortunately," said June, "I've found one entry that might throw some light on how Myra reacted."

This time I read the page before I copied it. It didn't do anything to change my growing contempt for Amos, although at least it showed that he knew how to be successful in what seemed to be his expanding business.

'Daddy has invited Mr Chevally again for today's sundowner and ordered me to be present. We will again take a quinine drink with tonic water and lime juice and perhaps a hard biscuit. It will be interesting to hear Mr Chevally's report of his business activities, of which Daddy so much approves. It appears that he has devised a form of beer that satisfies the taste of the soldiers more than the brews consumed heretofore. Apparently it has even been favourably received at some of our own socials. It is Daddy's opinion that Mr Chevally is likely to become a much richer man than he might have done had he remained at Home.'

"Looks to me," I said, "that Amos and Daddy are probably two sides of the same coin. Deceptive and unfeeling."

"And," June added, "Myra appears to be at the mercy of both of them."

"It would have been very interesting," I said, "to have been able to read what Myra thought of Amos the first time she met him. I'll bet whoever tore out some of the pages got rid of that entry."

"Here's one they didn't tear out," said June, handing me another page. It was a later entry, obviously, than the first two. As I read this one I gaped in amazement.

'I have gradually come to accept Amos for what he is. He is like the fruit of the pomegranate – on the outside, appealing, even sweet. On the inside, like the pomegranate seed, hard and impenetrable. He has, I believe, already asked Daddy for my hand although of me he has never

made the request. Not that it would make any difference as Daddy will accept the proposal for me anyway. I feel as though I am on the verge of a whole new life. I would so like to get away from this stifling atmosphere. Perhaps, with Amos, it may be possible, as he has told me that he has a brother who has gone to New South Wales. Surely there would be possibilities there that would satisfy his ambitions.'

Myra's metaphor of the pomegranate seed for her description of Amos left me speechless. Here were the very words I had heard in my head – twice – not exactly as Myra had written them, but with the same sentiment. The words of a woman who had accepted her fate and was prepared to make the best of it. The words of my great-grandmother.

June could see how affected I was by reading this diary entry. She leaned over and put her hand on my arm.

"Perhaps we should leave it there," she said gently.

I pulled myself together and answered her. "It explains so much," I said.

"It does," said June. "It explains how Myra was able to accept an arranged marriage. And it explains how she was willing to accept removal from India."

"And how she would have been prepared to advocate with Amos to go somewhere else," I said. "In fact, it may have been Myra who actually persuaded Amos to leave India and come here – don't you think? Not that he would ever have admitted that."

"What a blessing to have found these diary entries," said June. "They have told us so much."

"I have to say," I replied, "that it's been a bit overwhelming."

June smiled, and began carefully collecting the pages she had spread out on the table. "Let's go for a walk in the garden," she said. She secured the bundle of papers with a length of string and placed them in one of her filing cabinets. "We can come back another time, if you want to see more," she said.

"What about the races?" I said.

"We needn't hurry," she said. "I think that after looking at those pieces of what were really our great-grandmother's private thoughts, we've got a lot to reflect on."

That was certainly true. We left the building and walked out into the well-kept private garden at the back. As we strolled in wordless companionship I marveled at how our great-grandmother's thoughts, written down over a century ago and reflecting how she had felt about her situation in life, had brought June and me closer together.

I think it was then that I realised something about myself. I realised that there were changes that I needed to make. I needed to allow myself to be more aware of the feelings of others. I needed to allow myself to take more consideration of how other people felt. I felt overwhelmed by what seemed to be a new insight into myself.

"Let's sit here for awhile," said June, indicating an old-fashioned garden bench. The sun was high in the sky and the sounds of birds could be heard, coming from the nearby trees. As we sat down together, I wondered if perhaps Myra had once sat down on this bench and had thought about her life here, in a strange country, with a husband that – who knows? – she may by then have reconciled herself to.

As though she had read my thoughts, June said "Myra and the two children didn't come up from Sydney until Amos had the building finished. That I do know from the old records in the office."

"And how did she take to life here?" I asked. "Any indications in the diary?"

"Quite a few, actually," June replied. "There's a number of veiled statements about the relationship between Amos and Seth, and a rather touching description of a meeting with Agnes."

"So Amos actually allowed her to meet Agnes," I said.

"No, I don't think that was how it happened," June replied. "I think it was an initiative of Agnes, who would I'm sure have felt the responsibility of welcoming her sister-in-law to the district, whatever the relationship was between the brothers."

"And did Agnes and Myra get on?" I asked.

June smiled at the question. "Of course," she said.

I had to grin at that. "You said that because they

were both women," I said.

"Well," said June, "sometimes women understand, more than men do, what's important in life."

Instead of going over my head, or as they say, in one ear and out the other, as this remark would have usually done, it made me think. I sat there silently for awhile before I replied. I couldn't help remembering some of the relationships I'd had. Fiona, for example.

"I think," I said cautiously, "it depends on the woman. Not all women are as good at understanding things as others." I wanted to say, as you are for example. But I didn't.

"Well," said June, "what I understand is, that time is getting away and why don't we have a sandwich here before we set out for the races. That will save us having to scramble for lunch at the racecourse."

"Sounds great," I said.

"You wait here," said June. "I won't be a moment."

I relaxed on the garden bench. This was Myra's bench, I thought. Then I thought of her children – her daughter Margery, who I'd so recently discovered was my grandmother, with her brother, perhaps playing amongst these very garden beds while their mother looked on. How different this would have been from the life she grew up to in India.

Soon, June was as good as her word and appeared with sandwiches on a tray, which she set down on the bench between us. It was so peaceful that I could have happily stayed there for the whole afternoon.

June, however, was keen to get underway to the races. I didn't share her enthusiasm, but I wanted to share her company. And, I was wearing my new tweed jacket, and I'd had a haircut. I felt ready for anything. The sandwiches were finished.

"Just give me ten minutes," June said, scooping up the empty tray, and off she went.

Reading the bits of Myra's diary had given me so much to think about. For the first time I realised that this Royal Hotel, June's hotel, my great-grandfather Amos's hotel, would have been the childhood home of my grandmother Margery, daughter of Amos and Myra. What did Margery think of her father, I wondered. I recalled that last weekend, over at the family reunion, Muriel had announced to me that Margery had married a local free settler. Was it a marriage that Amos had arranged for her, I wondered, just as his marriage to Myra had been arranged?

My reverie was cut short by the reappearance of June. I can't remember now whether she had changed the dress she was wearing, but she had definitely added an extremely glamorous looking hat.

"Wow!" I exclaimed. "You look like a million dollars!"

She rewarded me with her wonderful smile. "Everybody likes to get dressed up for the Cup," she said.

"Let me drive you in my car," I said. June agreed, and soon we were on our way.

The road to the Murrendebri Racecourse was in the opposite direction to Melon Flats but quite close to the town and we soon arrived at the entry. Here, June handed me a card to show to the gatekeeper, who directed us to what he called the Members' Parking area. "What are you a member of?" I asked June.

"Why, the Murrendebri Picnic Race Club," she replied. "It's a club where members bring their own horse to the meeting, and often ride it themselves. It's very popular up this way. People come from miles around."

I'd never been interested in going to a race meeting in the city, but with what I'd learnt of the family history recently, something occurred to me right then, an observation that I just had to make.

"So," I said, "these Picnic Races here today are pretty much just like that meet in Staffordshire that Knottle told us about, that your ancestor Seth was so keen to take part in that he borrowed a horse without permission. And ended up here."

June looked amazed. "You know, I'd never thought of that before," she said. "Yes, I believe you're right. And that would have been why Seth established these meetings, years and years ago, and donated the land so that the racecourse could be set up. And the Picnic Races have been going ever since."

I'm going to have trouble describing the feeling

that came over me when I heard June say this. On the one hand, there was a warm glow because it seemed that something I'd said had helped her to understand something. An aspect of family history that she hadn't realised before. But underneath that was a darker feeling that I couldn't make sense of. Puzzling about it later, when I'd got back to Sydney, the closest I could come to identifying it was as a feeling of angry frustration – as though I'd been prevented from achieving a cherished ambition. It didn't make sense to me then, and it still doesn't.

But it didn't interfere with our enjoyment of watching the races. Of course June knew just about everybody, and one of the people who came up to say hello was the guy, Ralph, who had been in charge of the archery at the reunion the week before.

"Any time you want to improve your aim," he told me, "just contact me."

"Thanks," I said, but I think I'll give it a miss. I'm used to doing that."

June laughed at that and as Ralph moved away, she told me that he had made certain suggestions about modernising the hotel. "In fact," she said, "I think he's interested in buying into the business."

She looked away, and said in that remote voice of hers that I'd heard several times before, "If he made an offer, I'd be prepared to consider it."

It was a remark that she'd just thrown away, but to me it was a revelation. Did it mean that she might be prepared to leave Murrendebri? And if she did, would she ever consider the possibility of teaming up with me? Of becoming my partner? Perhaps even going the whole way, towards a permanent commitment?

I didn't dare reply to June's remark. Take it slowly, I warned myself. But somehow I knew that I had won June's confidence, and in my heart I rejoiced.

Suddenly, over the loudspeaker that had been announcing the races, came a voice that I recognised all too well.

"All ladies competing in the Best Hat Competition," barked the voice of Muriel, "come to the front of the Members' Stand. Judging will commence in five minutes."

"Don't tell me she's here," I said.

"Oh yes," June replied, "she's on the Committee. She's been judging the hat competition for years."

"Well," I said, "are you going in it? You should, you'll be bound to win."

June laughed. "I don't think so," she said. "I don't have the right pedigree."

"You surely don't mean," I said, "that Muriel never gives it to an Amos descendant?"

"Yes – usually a Seth descendant, or if not, an outsider," June informed me.

"Well." I burst out. "How stupid is that. Carrying on a feud that should have been forgotten years ago."

"Well, that's Muriel," said June simply. "After all – she hasn't had much in her life – up till now, that is, when she's developed her –er – friendship with Mr Knottle."

Before I knew it, I'd replied.

"Love changes people," was what I said.

A silence fell between us.

And suddenly, into my mind came again that mysterious quotation about the juice of the pomegranate lightening the heart for love. And just as suddenly it made some sense to me. I turned to June.

"Have you ever thought," I asked her, "what attracts people to each other?"

She thought for a minute. "No, I haven't," she said. "Have you?"

"Not till just now," I said. "But I think it is all tied up with what people need – what has been missing in their lives."

"How do you mean?" she replied.

"Well," I said, "look at what happens if you're thirsty. What you need is something to drink. And if you're – I don't know – emotionally thirsty, you need something sweet. Like – like – pomegranate juice."

"Pomegranate juice!" exclaimed June. "Is there any such thing?"

I knew that this was my chance to carry my feelings through, to give June some idea of how I felt about her.

"If I was a pomegranate," I commenced.

June dissolved in laughter. "Oh, you are funny," she said. "You – a pomegranate!"

"Yes," I said seriously. If I was – I'd be hard and unrelenting on the inside, but on the outside, I might be the kind of person that – that someone could love."

June's face was serious and I could tell that she understood what I'd meant, however badly I'd put it. Finally she spoke.

"I would need to know," she said, "more about the hard and unrelenting part."

"June," I said. "I think I'm in love with you."

CHAPTER 8

Love, it seems, has always been in the air

It's not the best place to tell someone that you love them – while standing in the middle of a crowd at the races, and just before the main race of the day was about to be run too. I knew immediately that I should have chosen a better time and place. But I guess that's always been me – if something needs to be said, I just say it. And I certainly needed right then to tell June how I felt about her.

As she stood there, looking so smart and glamorous, I couldn't tell what her reaction would be. After a moment she turned her head away and in that remote tone of voice that I was getting to know so well, she just said, "Thank you Roger, that's very sweet."

What could I make of that, I wondered. I desperately wanted to say more but in a way I also felt that I had already said everything.

This was when the events around us took over. After a crackling from the loud speaker, Muriel's voice resounded through the air, announcing the winner of the hat competition. "Congratulations to Debbie Maguire from Willow Vale," she pronounced.

June laughed then, and the awkwardness between us was dissipated. "An outsider, this year," she smiled. And then we heard the race commentator on the loud speaker announcing that the horses were lining up for the running of the Murrendebri Cup.

"Come on," said June, "let's try to find a spot on the rail so that we can see the race properly."

As I've said, I've never been interested in racing and on that day at the Murrendebri Picnic Races I had too much on my mind to give more than cursory attention to the race for the Cup that everyone around us was following with such absorption. But with June so eager to see it, I hurried with her to a spot where there was room for us to get a good view of the horses as they came thundering down the straight towards the finishing post.

I loved the way that June barracked for her favourite and felt her disappointment when it fell behind and lost, coming about fifth if I remember. "What a shame," she said, as the crowd began to disperse back into the paddock area. "That jockey was a Seth descendant, young John Richards from Willow Vale."

"Well," I said, "he's got a whole year to prepare for the next run. Better luck next time."

"Y-es," she said slowly. "As with most things – time will tell."

Somehow the way she said this gave my heart a boost. I remembered that I had offered to take her to dinner, and mentioned it to see if that was still what she wanted.

"Why of course," she said. "The new Indian restaurant. Why don't we go up there now – that's if you don't mind doing the driving."

I was more than happy to get out of the crowd, and we made our way to the car park.

It was easy to follow the road signs to Willow Vale and eventually we were on the winding road westward, driving into the face of the setting sun. June took off her fancy hat, and threw it over into the back seat.

I couldn't hold back any longer. "June," I said. "What I said to you earlier –" I got no further.

"Let's not talk about it now," June said. "Let's not spoil the evening."

That really set me back. All my earlier hopes seemed to crash and burn, like a devastated landscape. I couldn't say anything and concentrated on the road ahead.

After a silence that seemed to have lasted for a couple of miles, June turned to me and said, "Roger – I've had intimate friendships, as I know you have. I have my own life, as I know you have. We are two different people."

She paused then for a minute, then went on. "Even though we've known each other for a very short time, I think we have become very good friends. I know that's how I think of you, and I hope that's how you are able to think of me."

She paused again, and then continued. "But it seems to me that it would be silly to rush into a –" she hesitated for a moment – "a more complicated relationship. It could spoil the friendship we already have. And, honestly, that's something I wouldn't want to happen."

As I listened to this I puzzled over what it could mean for me in the days ahead. I tried to imagine what the situation between us looked like from June's point of view.

She'd mentioned having in the past what she had called intimate friendships. Was she still harboring feelings about one of these "friendships" that she hadn't quite let go of? I knew what that felt like from experiences of my own that I'd had in the past.

I felt I had to know the answer to this question. But wanting to know the answer to the question, and actually asking the question, were two different things. Fortunately, I think, I decided not to ask it – or at least, not just then.

It wasn't a long trip to Willow Vale and soon we were driving down what seemed to be the main street. Although the sun hadn't yet gone down, the atmosphere was gloomy with clouds gathering overhead. Just the night for a curry, I thought, and hoped that the place we were looking for would be as good as I'd hoped. Even though it had been recommended by Muriel.

It was easy to find the restaurant. A large sign proclaimed "Best Indian Curry – House of Bangalore". I parked in front and we got out of the car and went inside.

"Ah, welcome," said a very Indian looking gent. "Would you be wanting a table now for two."

In the old days – a week or so ago – I would probably have replied something like "that's about the size of it" but tonight, all that flippant side of me seemed to have fallen away and I just said, "Yes please" and followed as he led us to a very well situated table near the window, from where we could look out onto the street.

"Tonight," said the guy, who seemed to be our host, "we are having the very very special, the butter chicken cooked to perfection with steamed rice and coriander."

"I'd certainly like that," said June. She looked across the table at me. "What do you think?" she asked.

I couldn't help it, a line from a famous movie I'd

seen once jumped into my head. "I'll have what you're having," I said.

"Two butter chicken special," said the guy triumphantly, and he went off towards the kitchen.

A few other people had started to arrive and they were welcomed and seated nearby. I felt an urgent need to speak to June about how I felt. I looked into her eyes and stretched out my hand towards hers.

"June," I started. Then I faltered. I simply couldn't put what I felt into words.

"Roger," she said, "we're going to have lots of time to get to know each other really well. For now, this evening, let's just have a good time together. After all – what do you know about me? Or me about you? Rushed decisions are often mistaken decisions. Don't you think?"

"Does this mean that you'd like to see me again?" I asked. "After tonight, I mean?"

June smiled – that captivating smile. "Of course," she said.

I felt a burst of gratitude and I remember I replied "That's good enough for me," or words to that effect, and smiled back. I'd never felt so much at ease on what was actually a first date.

That was when our host came bustling up with a wine list which he thrust in front of me and before I could ask him anything he started on his spiel.

"You like nice wine with dinner," he informed me.

"We have all wines you like, red, white, sparkling, all local vineyards, also imported. You choose now?"

This seemed to me like a heavy sell and I looked at June to see how she was taking it.

I could see that she was amused. "I think," she said, "that a little rosé would be nice."

"That's what we'll have," I said, handing back the wine list. "A bottle of your best rosé."

This didn't throw the guy for a minute. "Local or import?" he wanted to know.

To tell you the truth, I wasn't all that used to ordering wine with dinner. It had been one of the points of contention with Fiona, as well as some of my previous dates, because I was usually happy with a beer. I think June must have seen my indecision and covered it for me.

"Local, please," she informed the guy, naming a particular local vineyard.

"Ah! We have. I get," he replied, and hurried off.

"I know the winemaker there," June informed me. "We often serve his wines when we have to cater for special parties."

"Well," I said, "you learn something every day."

"Yes," said June, who was looking out the window, "and we're probably going to have to learn a lot more in a minute."

I followed her gaze. And there, parking in front of my car, was Knottle on his motor bike, with Muriel's car pulled up in the street next to him. Through the window, we could see Muriel giving him directions about how to park his bike.

"Surely they're not coming here," I said.

"I think so," said June. "Muriel will probably want to make some comment to us about our Indian ancestry —slight though it is, after how many generations?"

I wasn't sure. "Quite a few, now," was all I could think of to say.

Sure enough, a few minutes later there was a commotion at the door, which was Muriel making her entrance. "My word," she announced to the host who had hurried to greet her, "you people have done wonders with this awful run-down old shop. "Why, it could be anywhere in India."

"Memsahib," said the host, bowing deeply, "come this way. For you we have the special table."

"Come along, Phineas," Muriel called behind her, and Knottle obediently followed her to where she was being led — right up to the table next to us.

"What a surprise!" she proclaimed as she approached us. But I knew it wasn't.

June rose to the occasion. "It is a surprise, isn't it," she said to Muriel. "We weren't expecting to see you either."

"Well," said Muriel, seating herself, "I thought I should come and see how you're adjusting to your Indian ancestry. That which Phineas," as she graciously waved Knottle to the seat opposite her, "has discovered for you."

"We're thrilled about it," I said. "So much more interesting that just having a convict in the family."

I didn't expect June to intervene, but I can see now why she did.

"We're a family, Muriel," she said, "and for me, a family accepts everyone who belongs to it for what they are."

She didn't say any more, but I could see that Muriel knew that this was a veiled criticism of her attitude. Without replying to June she called over the host and said "Mr Knottle and I will have tonight's special, thank you." The host guy bowed deeply again and hurried off.

What June had just said about being a family had made me aware that my attitude to Muriel and her friend Knottle probably needed some adjustment. Particularly as it seemed that they were about to have their dinner at the next table. I turned towards Knottle and tried to think of something friendly to say. As nothing suitable seemed to come to mind, I was relieved when he spoke first.

"Researching your family," he said to me, "has been one of the most interesting projects I have ever undertaken."

It happens sometimes when you start to talk to people, you begin to feel interested. "Do you do this sort of thing all the time?" I asked him.

"No," Knottle replied. "I'm usually –"

He was interrupted by Muriel, who declared loudly enough to be heard several tables away, "Phineas is the librarian in charge at the Murrendebri Municipal Library."

"So you're really a librarian," I said to him.

Knottle hesitated a bit before he answered. "Yes," he said, "but with an interest in local history."

"And, in Murrendebri," interrupted Muriel, "that means an interest in the most interesting local family – the Chevalleys."

June told me later how relieved she was that I didn't respond to this challenging remark of Muriel's. I just ignored it and went on talking to Knottle.

"You must have discovered just about everything about this family by now," I said.

"Oh no," Knottle replied. "There's that old story about Amos's treasure that I haven't even begun to explore."

"No truth in that story at all," Muriel snorted. "If Amos had left that sort of thing, it would have come to light years ago."

"Not necessarily," said Knottle. As he looked directly at Muriel I was almost sure that I saw his backbone stiffen. "These old stories, while they may have altered during the years, seem always to have a basis of truth," he said.

I was warming to this guy. How many times, when assessing insurance claims, had I set out to find the truth of a story that some client had tried to put over the company. Very often, I had found, there was a truth at the bottom of the story but it had been manipulated out of all recognition.

"So, do you have a theory?" I asked him. "Did Amos leave some hidden valuable behind, or is it a figment of someone's imagination?"

"The only theory I have," said Knottle, "is that Amos did leave behind something, in all likelihood something that he himself treasured. That may not mean," he continued, "that it would have been equally regarded by other people. Members of his family, for instance."

I found this an interesting thought. After all, I reminded myself, we're talking about my great-grandfather, and who knows what he might have regarded as valuable, except perhaps money.

Muriel hadn't been able to break into the conversation and was like a horse champing at the bit. "Stuff and nonsense," she barked. "Amos was a mean old so-and-so who would have made sure that he didn't leave behind anything helpful. Whereas Seth," she proclaimed, "provided for all his children and died a highly regarded citizen of Murrendebri and the whole district."

Fortunately at this point, dinner arrived for June and me and the conversation was suspended. After delivering our plates, the host hovered around offering various side dishes to go with our chicken curry which, in his words, would 'let the spices say very much hello to your stomach and carry you halfway to heaven', or words more or less to that effect.

I found this a bit too exotic to take seriously but luckily June interrupted his flow by saying "Just a cucumber and coconut sambal, please. That's all," and he hurried away to the kitchen to supply it.

"How did you know what to order?" I asked June.

"I didn't", she laughed, "but at least I recognised cucumber and coconut, so I think we'll be fairly safe with whatever arrives."

As our meal progressed, and Muriel and Knottle received theirs, I couldn't help wondering if this was like the food that Amos would have eaten when he went to Bengal. Would he have missed the traditional English roast beef, I wondered; and, alternatively, when she came here, would Myra have missed the kind of dishes that she would have been provided at home in India.

Somehow for me this threw a new light on their relationship. The pair of them, each in their own way, I decided, were culturally dislodged. A situation that each would have been able to recognise in the other. Maybe, I speculated, that might have been what made a relationship between them possible.

I realised that I had started to think about relationships in a way that was new to me. Things that might make relationships between people work, and things that mightn't. Was it having a chicken curry in this faux Indian environment that had done this? No. It was how I felt about June, and how I wanted to be sure that I didn't do anything to jeopardise the relationship with her that I so much aspired to.

Now we were finishing our meal, and at the next table Muriel and Knottle were still tucking in. I felt strongly that we should try to get away before they finished, to avoid any complications. I said quietly to June, "should we go now?"

"I'm done," she replied. So I signed to the host, who came galloping up with another menu, this time with Indian sweets on it. "We have for you tonight," he proclaimed, "the coconut milk oat pudding. Very very nice."

"No, just the bill, thanks," I said. Apparently this was too much for Muriel to ignore. She leaned over towards us. "Phineas and I," she said, "will be having the pudding."

It surprised me to find that I wasn't annoyed by this intrusion of Muriel's, as I had always been in the past. In fact, as I looked at her and Knottle, sitting there enjoying their Indian meal, an unaccustomed feeling that I can only describe as benevolence came over me. After all, I reasoned, Muriel was a relation of June's, and now I come to think of it, of mine too. If I was going to be guided by what June had said earlier, about

137

accepting family people for what they were, I could very well start here. That's why all I said was, "Sorry we can't stay. Enjoy yourselves."

June and I left our table and I paid at the reception desk on the way out. "You come again, Sahib," the bloke said, bowing as he accepted my credit card. Somewhere inside me, my old self said "I can do without the bullshit, thanks mate," but that stayed inside me and I just thanked him for giving us his much appreciated attention.

As I negotiated my car away from Knottle's motor bike and we started on the drive back to Murrendebri, June suddenly said "What did you make of what Mr Knottle – Phineas – said about Amos's treasure? That it could very well exist, and that it might be something that meant something special to him, but not necessarily to others?"

I don't know if what happened then was because of being with June on our first date. Maybe having enjoyed what I had to admit was an excellent Indian meal might have had something to do with it. Or, was it having sort of got over the feeling of belligerence that Muriel had always produced in me? Maybe it was a coalescence of all of these positive factors. Whatever it was, something stirred in me. I can only try to describe it by saying it was like a light going on somewhere.

The sort of guy that Amos must have been was suddenly very familiar. When I think about it now, I can see that there were a few points in my own life where it would be easy to relate to a guy like Amos and this is probably what happened that night – on the drive back to what after all had been Amos's home, the Royal (Empire) Hotel in Murrendebri.

"Look," I said to June, "Amos didn't take kindly to his young brother being more capable and more likeable than him. And when he realised that the girl he fancied didn't want a bar of him, because she was in love with his young brother, he was incensed."

"But even if he was," said June, "he shouldn't have called the police. After all, Seth was going to take the horse back to the livery stables – it needn't have been a case of theft."

"I don't know who called the police," I said, "but I know that it wasn't Amos." Something inside me told me that this was the truth. "It could have been any one of the others," I said. "Maybe even the squire's brother – that rotten Colonel back from India who tried to seduce Agnes. I wouldn't have put it past him to try to get Seth out of the way."

"Even though he's your great-great grandfather?" June wanted to know.

"From what I can gather," I said, "there's a bad egg in every family. And it's not who you're descended from that makes you who you are. That's your own responsibility. Why, I think you told me that yourself."

"I certainly think that," June said. "And that's why I'm glad that you're one of the good eggs."

This was such a frank and unexpected statement that I took my eyes off the road for a moment to look at

June. Even in the dim inside light of the car I could see that she was smiling warmly.

We didn't say much more on the trip back to the hotel. Somehow we didn't have to – a mutual understanding had been established and for me the world shone in a golden glow.

As we pulled up in front of the Royal I realised that I still hadn't found out exactly where June lived in the rambling premises. I felt that she wouldn't misunderstand me if I asked her. So I did.

"Why," she said, "I've got the flat behind the kitchen that my grandfather built when he modernised the place. According to my father, Grandfather said that he wasn't going to live in the same rooms that Amos had spent his life here in."

"You mean the one I'm in – No.1," I said.

"Well yes," said June, "but apparently he allowed Myra to have No.1, which was big enough for her and the children. He went next door, to No.2. So for Grandfather, both No.1 and No.2 were no-no's."

You'd probably think that my reaction to this information would have been a repeat of the creepy feelings I'd had on different occasions to both these rooms but it wasn't like that at all. I felt an overwhelming sense of peace and somewhere inside, a feeling that at last I'd understood something about my great-grandparents that had been eluding me. I realised that they had made a life together, on their own terms – just as everybody has to, I suppose, if they are to have a life at all.

I felt June's hand on my arm. "See you at breakfast," she said, as she reached over to the back seat for her hat and opened the car door. In an instant she had disappeared into the hotel and, after locking my car, I followed and went up the stairs to No.1.

The only feeling I had was, that I was coming home. I was ready for bed in no time and knew no more until a ray of sunshine crossed my face in the morning.

CHAPTER 9

The fate of the Royal Hotel is decided but am I happy about it?

My first thought that Sunday morning was that my visit to Murrendebri would have to finish today. June had invited me to come up for the races and that had happened yesterday.

Before I left this morning though I would have to think of some way to suggest seeing her again. I realised that I could hardly invite myself to keep driving up from Sydney and staying at the hotel.

Maybe, I thought, she might find it possible to come to Sydney sometime? But if she did, would she want to stay with me, at my place? Remembering our conversation last night, I didn't think that was a suggestion I should make. At least – not yet. But in the future? I hurried out of bed, showered quickly and hurried downstairs to the dining room.

June met me at the door as before, but this time she didn't ask me how I'd slept or anything. "Roger," she said, "is there any reason you have to leave today?"

"Why no, I suppose not," I said. "I've got some time off from work –"

June interrupted me. "Then I hope you'll stay on for awhile," she said, "I'd value your opinion about something. And don't forget – we still haven't looked at all the surviving pieces of Myra's diary. Would you like to do that?"

"Would I ever," I said.

"Then come along to the office after breakfast," June said. "Go on in, I've already ordered your bacon and eggs." And with that, she went off, not into the dining room, but back towards the office.

As I enjoyed breakfast, I relished in the pleasure that June's words had given me. That she should value my opinion about anything was a complete surprise. I didn't waste time wondering what it was going to be about and refusing the offer of a second cup of coffee I hurried along to June's office.

I half expected her to have the pieces of Myra's diary out on the side table, as she had last time, but this was different. Sitting with June at the desk was a familiar face – the man who'd offered me archery coaching, Ralph Chevally.

I remembered immediately something that June had mentioned about Ralph having offered suggestions about modernising the hotel. I felt an inward flush of pride that June apparently wanted me to give an opinion about whatever the proposal was.

It was an odd moment for me – in a funny sort of way, to think that I might be involved in the fate of the hotel that my great-grandfather had built. Somehow it put the seal on my membership of this so recently discovered family. In a word, it suddenly made me feel that I belonged.

"I'm glad you're still here, Roger," said Ralph. "I think June's a bit hesitant about some of the details I've suggested for the hotel. Maybe it would help if we could talk it over with a third party."

I shot a quick look at June before replying, and the look on her face told me all I needed to know.

"Go ahead. I'm all ears," I told Ralph. He immediately went into details.

"There's a big tourist potential up here," he commenced. "There's a couple of new vineyards that are doing very well – as June knows – but now there's news of something bigger. A mate of mine in the racing industry –"

"Not a cousin?" June put in. Ralph grinned.

"No," he said, "not everyone up here's a Chevally.

This guy's a financial advisor to one of the big racing conglomerates, they've got breeding stables down in the southern highlands and they want to establish one up here. Apparently they've found that the Murrendebri Racecourse is a perfect training circuit and they've approached the Jockey Club with a mutually beneficial proposal, to ally it with their proposed development."

"That's the racecourse that was originally designed by Seth," June stated. There was a tone of modest pride in her voice as she said this.

Ralph grinned. "Yes," he said, "don't mention that to Muriel. So that's why I think it's time to think about refurbishing this old place, to make it more attractive to the inflow of visitors that the new development it likely to attract."

Ralph paused and looked at June for a reaction.

"When you say refurbishment," she said, "is there any indication of what sort of cost would be involved?"

"That would depend on what was done, of course," Ralph said. "But I can't see the point of half measures. Either go the whole hog and end up with the best accommodation Murrendebri has to offer, or don't bother."

"Well," said June, "the hotel has been virtually untouched since Grandfather's renovation, when amongst other things he added the balcony on the front. I would really like to see it brought up-to-date as you suggest. But I think that would have to mean a change in ownership."

145

"I can see that," said Ralph, "and that's why I'm going to put before you a suggestion that I hope you'll find it impossible to refuse."

I'd sat silently until now. But Ralph's words carried a certain undertone that in all my years as a claims assessor I had learned to recognise. It was the voice of someone putting forward a proposal which claimed to be a benefit but which was in fact a benefit for the proposer.

"Hang on a bit," I said. There was no point in mincing words. "Are you suggesting that you want to buy June out?"

I recognised then that Ralph was what we call in the business a smooth operator.

"Oh!" he exclaimed. "Only on terms that would be the most favourable for her, of course."

I'm not a businessman, but a life as a claims assessor has given me a nose that seems to automatically smell out self-interest. There was a perceptible whiff of it in the air right now.

"So if June would no longer own the Royal," I said – slowly, so that Ralph wouldn't know that I was already onto him – "if she didn't own it, who would run it?"

"Oh, that would be a question that the Board would have to answer," he replied.

"Board? What Board?" I asked.

"Yes!" June chipped in. "Who are these mysterious people you're talking about, Ralph?"

"Well," said Ralph, "if this goes ahead it would be a major business enterprise, so naturally, people who put their money into it would want to have a voice."

"And who are these people?" June asked again.

"They're a group of investors," Ralph began, who've asked me to –" he suddenly paused.

And as he did so the whole scenario was plain to see in front of me. I could see no point in holding back.

"Have these people by any chance approached you, and asked you to chair the Board of the company you're forming?" I asked Ralph, in as guileless a voice as I could manage.

What followed was the inevitable roundabout explanation that leads nowhere when people want to avoid answering a question. To quote the replies he gave us, Ralph 'couldn't say what the Board would decide'; – they were after all 'individual members who would each have their own opinion'; and – 'nothing could be decided until the proper procedures had been followed'. In short – he effectively avoided answering my question. And that, despite his roundabout reply, provided the answer I needed.

He'd been offered the job, if the deal came off. I knew it as definitely as if he'd said it himself.

June leant back in her chair. "Well," she said. "Running the hotel isn't exactly a bed of roses. There's always a problem that needs to be solved, and when that's done, there always seems to be another one just around the corner. How would this Board of yours know how to pick the right person for the job?"

"It seems to me," I said, sounding as naïve as possible, "that they'd probably have to leave the decision to their Chairman. Whoever it might turn out to be, of course."

To give him his due, Ralph laughed at that. He could tell that what I'd said was directed at him. When he spoke, there was a change in his manner.

"Look," he said, "it's true that there is interest in the hotel. Interest from people with big money to spend. They've got assets in all the big tourist areas, from the Queensland Gold Coast to the Victorian snowfields. And it's also true, as Roger has been astute enough to realise, that part of their proposal includes appointing me to head the development."

I couldn't resist it. "A bit the same as an offer that was once made to your ancestor Amos," I said.

"Eh?" said Ralph. I could tell that he couldn't make the connection. But June could.

"Amos sold out his brother," she said simply. "And because of it, he had to live the rest of his life in the shadow of that betrayal."

"Oh, that old story," said Ralph.

I'm not usually given to making profound statements, but on looking back, I think what I said next was the exception.

"Sometimes, what people do in their life," I said, "stays around for much longer than they do."

June knew exactly what I meant. She nodded.

"And what they've done affects the lives of other people who come after them," she added to what I'd said.

There was silence for awhile then. It was as though none of the three of us wanted to continue the line of thinking that Ralph had introduced. It was Ralph himself who spoke first.

"Getting back to the idea I had to put before you, It's one thing to develop a first class tourist facility, like a luxury hotel," he said. "But it's quite another thing to fill it with customers."

"Exactly," said June. "How do we know whether this new racehorse training facility, if that's what it is, will bring swarms of visitors to Murrendebri? I don't see it as being likely at all."

"It would have to be an enormous marketing exercise," said Ralph, "and it's hard to tell how successful it might be – or might not be."

That was when I picked up where Ralph really stood in this matter. He'd had a tempting offer from these mysterious backers he'd told us about, so tempting that he wanted to give it the fullest consideration, but underneath the enticement he also felt the reservation that June's comment had just brought out into the open.

I felt then I had to help them both to find the common ground that lay between them.

"You know what," I said. "You might not have to renovate the whole hotel. You've already got a first-class dining room – at least, the breakfast is first class. Why not extend the menu, and serve lunches and dinners? Then people wouldn't have to go up to Willow Vale –"

June laughed. "For an Indian meal," she chuckled. "Yes, I'm sure we could do that. Our young chef is dying to expand what he's able to offer from the kitchen. I could talk to him today, and sound him out about it."

"That might be a good move," said Ralph cautiously, "but it's no good having a good restaurant if you can't offer first class accommodation to go with it."

"Well," said June, "as Roger has just said, we might not have to renovate the whole place."

"It won't be an easy job," said Ralph. "For a start, you've got that communal bathroom. That would have to go."

I had to laugh. "I used that bathroom the first night I was here," I said. "It took me about ten minutes to work out how to use the shower. I reckon it should be preserved as an antique."

Ralph didn't see the joke. "These days," he said, "people expect an en-suite. You'd have to carve up some of the rooms and use the spaces to install private facilities for every bedroom."

"That would mean an enormous plumbing job, as

well as the other building adjustments," said June. "The cost would be huge. And anyway, we wouldn't need to modernise every room. The old bathroom could stay to service the rooms we don't renovate."

"Well," said Ralph, "that might work, just as long as you've got something really classy to offer the kind of people who might want that level of accommodation."

"Simple," said June. "If people ring up and want a superior room, and we already have people booked into that room, then what we have to do is say we're very sorry, but we're booked out at that level."

"That raises the question," said Ralph, "of how many rooms you want to modernise."

"Yes," said June. "That is a very sobering question. The hotel doesn't have cash reserves to draw on. We would have to make some arrangement in order to finance the renovation, no matter how small-scale we manage to make it."

Another silence descended on us but I could see that Ralph was working something over in his mind. Eventually he spoke.

"What I'm going to say," he said, "I want you to know that it's got nothing to do with the scheme I told you about earlier."

"You mean those mysterious backers you were talking about?" said June.

"That's right," Ralph replied. "This is my idea and it's a genuine offer that I hope you'll want to consider."

"So, it isn't one of those offers you can't refuse?" I said. I'd intended this remark to be humorous. Ralph didn't get the joke but June did. She gave me one of her smiles and said, "I'm so glad you were able to stay, Roger, and help with this. It's really made a difference to have your view on things."

What I felt like saying was "I'd be willing to stay with you forever" but I had the good sense to keep that sentiment to myself.

What I did say was "No worries."

Then I added, "And, I've been thinking about this modernisation problem."

"That's what I want to talk about," said Roger. He fixed me with a very firm look. "And it certainly isn't one of those offers you can't refuse. This is my offer and no-one else is involved in it. And June," he said, transferring his gaze from me to her, "I want you to know that it's genuine with no hidden complications. What I'm proposing is for me to finance the renovations in return for a share in the ownership."

There was silence in the room. It was like when you chuck a rock into a pond, there's the initial splash and then you watch the ripples silently spread out towards the edge. I wondered how June was going to react and waited silently for her response.

"Have you got the money to do that?" she asked eventually.

"Well," Ralph replied, "it would depend on how

big the job turns out to be. But I'd be prepared to go into debt to see it done, because I think that's what the place needs."

"Yes, I can see that," June replied, "it's what the times require. Old places like the Royal have to keep up-to-date or they just have to close and are lost forever."

"That's what we have to prevent," Ralph said, "and I'm prepared to help make sure it doesn't happen."

As I sat there listening to this conversation between cousins, not even conscious of the fact that I was a cousin too, I seemed to hear, somewhere deep inside of me, indistinctly but very definitely, a voice that I had heard before. Like a whisper in the wind, came the words 'the juice of the pomegranate….'

That was all, and then it was gone. But my instinct told me that it was a message – who from, and why, I didn't know, but I felt inside of me a deep sense of satisfaction. I knew that things in that room had taken the right turning.

I didn't know whether to say anything or not. There was an easy silence amongst the three of us and I decided to wait for one of the others to speak first.

It was June who broke the silence.

"Ralph," she said. "It's been something like seven years since I inherited the Royal from my father. As you know, I was an only child so it had to come to me. To tell you the truth, if I had been able to choose, I would have gone in a different direction but I've done the best

I could. But it isn't something that I can't share with someone else. Or even," and here she hesitated and lowered her eyes, "or even give up completely."

"So you're willing to consider an offer?" said Ralph.

"I am willing to consider it, and I'm interested in it, but I need a little time to think about it," she said.

"Of course you do!" Ralph exclaimed. "There'll be a lot of details to work out, if you decide to go with the idea. We'd have to consider all sorts of things, like who would hold the hotel license, how much of a share you'd be willing to release, whether you'd want other family members involved —"

June interrupted him. "This is all too much to start thinking about at this stage," she said. "Besides, I would first like to come to a decision about renovating, and what scale of renovation would be best for us to consider."

I didn't want to push myself into a conversation where I wasn't wanted, but from what I'd heard earlier, there was a very simple observation that needed to be made, right then.

"If," I said, "as Ralph has said before, he could finance a relatively modest renovation that might only involve a few rooms, wouldn't that relieve the —" I chose my words carefully — "the new partnership — of needing to go into debt?"

Ralph turned to me. "That's good thinking,"

he said seriously. "I reckon you've hit the mark there, Roger!"

"And I didn't need coaching," I replied, trying to keep it light-hearted, which I could see he appreciated.

"If we just did a small internal renovation," Ralph observed, "we wouldn't need official approval and we could probably find good enough tradesmen here in Murrendebri to get the job done."

"So what's stopping us?" I said.

I suddenly realised that by saying that, without thinking, I'd included myself in the arrangement. I wasn't part of this collaboration and I should have kept my nose out of it. I tried to back-peddle but June stopped me.

"Roger," she said, "I hope you'll always feel at home here. After all, this was home to your great-grandparents – Amos and Myra. And I know that your grandmother, Margery, was brought up here. She would have gone off to school from here every day, and come home here in the afternoons. This is every bit your emotional home as it is ours," and she looked at Ralph for confirmation.

"I don't go in for that stuff like you do, June," he said, "but I can see what you mean, because that's how I felt when it occurred to me that the old place might have to close down unless we could do something to improve it."

It was now that a thought that had been hovering

at the back of my mind brought itself forward.

"You know what," I said. "If you wanted a couple of first-class en-suite rooms, probably at not too much cost, there's an easy way to do it."

"Tell us!" said June.

"Well," I said, "I've stayed in both No. 1 and No. 2. And, I can pretty much assure you, they're not haunted."

"That's a pity," said Ralph. "Could be a good selling point."

I wasn't sure if Ralph was serious or not, but I continued. "They were the two rooms that Amos and Myra made their private quarters."

"Yes!" said June. "That's why Grandfather built the flat I've been living in. Apparently he said he wasn't going to share his life with memories he'd rather forget."

"Amos had a big bathroom opening off No. 1," I said, "and it's situated right between No. 1 and No. 2. What if we —" I got no further.

"Cut it in two, and make an en-suite for No. 2 out of it, as well as for No. 1!" exclaimed Ralph.

"That's exactly what I was thinking," I said.

June clapped her hands. "The perfect solution!" she cried.

"And," said Ralph, "probably not too difficult a job for a couple of good local tradesmen. I reckon it could be a winner all round."

"Right," said June. She was suddenly the competent businesswoman, in control of the situation. "Ralph – you and I will go straight away to see our accountant. His office is just up the street. I want us both to be able to agree on the terms of this new arrangement. As soon as that's done, we can discuss who we'll give the job to." She turned to me.

"Roger," she said, "you've helped so much with this. You told me that you've got time off work. Why not stay for a few days, until we get this project properly sorted out and under way?"

I think I probably stuttered a bit as I replied, it was such a sudden and such a welcome invitation. "I – I'd love to," I said. "Thank you."

"Now," said June, "come along Ralph, we'll go down to my accountant's office. And Roger,' she said, "why don't you go and wait for us in the lounge. There'll be no-one there at this hour, and when we come back, I want the three of us to have a celebratory drink together to seal this wonderful family agreement. There's a bottle of champagne I've been keeping in the bar and I'll bring it along as we come back."

A glass of champagne at this hour of the morning? I thought, if June pours it out – Why not! Yes please!

June and Ralph hurried off together and I strolled down the corridor towards the lounge to wait for them to come back.

Like an echo, those words returned to my thoughts. 'The juice of the pomegranate' was whispered

157

somewhere in my brain.

I knew then that the feelings that June and I were discovering for each other heralded a permanent relationship. I felt a happiness I had never known before.

CHAPTER 10

Sparkling Shiraz seals the deal

I wasn't in a hurry to go and wait in the lounge, I knew that June and Ralph would be away at the accountant's for some time so instead, I walked out into the private garden at the back and sat down on the bench that I had begun to think of as Myra's seat. There was a lot of thinking I had to do.

June lived here, in Murrendebri. I lived in Sydney. How, I wondered, would we ever be able to sustain the kind of relationship I was looking forward to, over this sort of distance?

I know that people do – but how well can they

cope without each other – sometimes for weeks, or even months? No – there had to be a solution and I was determined that I was going to try and find it.

But as I thought over the problem more and more, I finally realised that it was a problem that the two of us would share, and therefore, the two of us would need to solve the problem together. Thinking about it on my own was getting me nowhere.

Time had moved on. I got up and returned to the hotel and walked into the lounge to wait for June and Ralph. Soon I could hear them coming down the corridor from the bar, June in high spirits as, coming into the lounge, she explained what had happened to the bottle of champagne she had wanted to open for us.

"Sam, the barman," she laughed, "opened it last night for a group of four friends celebrating a 21st birthday, and they drank the lot."

"But," added Ralph, "he's given us this to try instead."

'This' was a bottle identified on its label as Sparkling Shiraz. "Well," I said, "it says Shiraz. If that's a red wine, I'm prepared to give it a go."

"It's from one of the local vineyards," said Ralph, "so it should be interesting. Sam thought we should at least give it a try."

He popped the cork and poured our drinks into the glasses June had brought from the bar. The wine was certainly red, richly coloured and fizzing furiously.

It reminded me of the last time I had taken a sip of sparkling wine, during that last disastrous dinner with Fiona. I decided that was a memory best forgotten.

Ralph tasted the sparkling shiraz. "H'm," he observed. "Could be the next wine fad. We could promote this here at the Royal! What about it, June?"

"Here's to the future," cried June. We clinked our glasses and I took an exploratory sip. Pleasantly surprised, I said "Well, if the future's as good as this, we've got nothing to worry about."

June gave me one of her brilliant smiles. And that was when she explained to me the understanding that she and Ralph had come to about the future of the hotel.

In brief, this was the arrangement. "Ralph is going to buy me out," she said, "partly by covering the cost of the renovation we've agreed on, and partly in terms of the residual valuation when the renovation's finished."

I have to say this gave me quite a shock. I hadn't realised that June would have wanted so readily to shed her possession of the hotel that she'd inherited from her father, and run as the great-grand-daughter of the man who'd built it.

"Are you sure that's what you want?" I asked her. Then, I thought to myself, what will she do instead, when she's not running the Royal – and that was a question that I felt was too delicate to ask her just yet.

But as it turned out, I didn't have to ask the question. June supplied the information without hesitation. She put down her glass and sat down on the nearby lounge. Ralph and I took the cue and sat down too.

"If I'd had a choice, I wouldn't have chosen to run the hotel. It was really because I was Dad's only child," she commenced. "He was a great manager, and taught me so well that when he died, I just slipped into the job – partly, I think, as a way of commemorating his memory."

She paused. "But I'd always had a yearning to express myself differently." She paused again. "I don't suppose you've noticed a few of the paintings around the walls here?"

Ralph and I followed her gesture. There were about five or six art works on the walls – I knew so little then that I didn't know whether they were done in oils or watercolour but what I did know was that they were all scenes of peaceful valley views, with distant hills and fertile looking creek flats – a bit like the scene at Melon Flats where we'd had the family reunion.

'You painted these?" I gasped.

June smiled. "In my spare time," she said.

Now I understood. "What you really wanted to do instead of managing the hotel was to train as an artist," I said. "Was that it?"

"Yes it was," she said, "and this arrangement with Ralph is going to make it possible for me to do it after all."

Ralph grinned proudly. "And it will allow me," he

said, "to do something I've always wanted – to run the business here at the Royal."

It took awhile for me to take in June's revelation. I knew nothing about art, except that if you were famous, your work could sell for some very high prices. I'd recently had to assess a claim that involved a painting that had been damaged in a house fire and I'd had to interview a couple of art critics to get reliable information about it. I realised that I'd probably have to spend a bit of time getting to know more about the art scene, if June was to get involved in it.

Ralph, however, was keen to discuss the proposed renovation and that's where the conversation went.

"There's a couple of guys up here who've got a business going between them," he told us. "One's a plumber and his mate's a carpenter. I reckon they might be able to handle a job like this."

"You don't mean Troy and Jayden, do you?" asked June.

"Yep," Ralph replied, "I've seen some of their work, they're a good team."

June laughed. "They're also regulars in the bar," she said.

"Well, that's good," I said. "They'll have a personal interest in the place."

"I'll give them a ring on their mobile later," said Ralph.

"Which one do you have to speak to?" June asked.

"Doesn't matter," Ralph replied, "they've only got the one mobile. They live together, if you know what I mean."

That seemed to finish the conversation. June said she wanted to sound out the chef about expanding the menu, and Ralph went off to do some measurements before ringing his builder pals.

"If you've really got the rest of the week free," June said to me, "why don't you stay on until Ralph gets the renovations organised?"

I felt my pulse starting to race. This was more than I'd hoped for.

"We'll probably have to move you out of No.1," she said, "but if you'd be happy to take one of the smaller rooms, we can organise that today. Why not come with me now, while we have a chat to the chef."

As we went through the dining room towards the kitchen, June told me a bit about the chef. "He's from New Zealand," she said, "here on a twelve month working visa but keen to stay on when that expires. So he figured he could get a job with more responsibility if he went somewhere up the country, rather than get work in Sydney. So I hope he'll come on board with what I'm going to suggest."

It was the first time I'd seen June in her managerial role and I could see how well she did it. She first suggested the expansion of the menu to include lunches and dinners, and listened to the guy's reaction – which was, in short, that with the minimal staff they had in the kitchen, it would be hard to do both extra meals without taking on another hand.

"But," he said, "most tourists won't want to stay in the hotel for lunch. Why don't we skip that, and just offer them a really gourmet dinner. We can certainly cope with that."

June immediately saw both the reality and the attraction of his suggestion and agreed to it without any further discussion. With that decided, we went back towards the office and as we did so June said, "You know that there's still some of Myra's diary you haven't seen. Why don't we take a look at it now?"

"I seem to have been thinking about her a lot today," I said, as we walked into the office.

"There's a couple of pages in particular that I think you should look at," June told me. "I won't say anything more until you've read them but I really would like to know what you think they mean."

This intrigued me a lot and I sat down while June got the diary out of its hiding place in one of her filing cabinets. She undid it and began to lay the pieces out on the small table, as she had done the first time.

I noticed again how beautiful Myra's handwriting was. Whatever else her father hadn't done for her, he must have seen to it that she had a good education.

"Start with this one," said June, placing a page in

front of me. This is what it said.

And the traveller shook off her cloak and sat down in front of her host.

'You are weary after your journey,' said the host. 'Will you take a little refreshment?'

'Thank you,' the traveller said. 'I am a long way from my home and much of my journey still lies ahead of me.'

'Is it a journey that you have undertaken freely, of your own free will?' asked the host. 'Or is it a journey that has been imposed upon you?'

The traveller smiled. 'It is both,' she said. 'But I do not expect you to understand this.'

'What I do understand,' said the host,' is that your journey is a painful one. And a lonely one, too, as you have no travelling companion.'

'Ah,' said the traveller, 'I do have a travelling companion. You do not see him, but he is with me always – in my mind.'

'But only in your mind?' asked the host. 'Surely, if he is a true companion, he must travel with you in your heart as well.'

'I would take him to my heart,' said the traveller, 'if his heart would allow it. But his heart is hard – like the seed of the pomegranate.'

'Even the seed of the pomegranate will one day crack and open,' said the host.

'That day,' said the traveller, *'is the day when my journey will have come to its end.'*

I finished reading and sat in amazement.

"Well," said June, "what do you make of it?"

All I could do was shake my head. The words Myra had written seemed to have woken an echo in my brain.

Finally I tried to put into words the effect that this page of Myra's diary had had on me.

"It's like a code," I said. That was the only way I could describe it. "Myra has written it as a story – or part of a story – but it has a hidden meaning. What it's really about," I said, "is her relationship with Amos."

As I said this, I had a most uncanny feeling. I felt that I knew Myra my great-grandmother personally, that she was a real person to me, that in some weird way she was with us in the room, that what she had written came from her heart and that I was interpreting this unusual diary entry of hers absolutely correctly.

"Amos seems hard-hearted," I continued, "but she knows that somewhere there is a key to opening what he feels in his heart and she will go on searching until she finds that key."

"In a way, then, she must have grown to love him for what he was," said June.

"There's more to it," I said. "She did grow to love him, but he grew to love her too – in his own way, perhaps, but what love he was capable of giving, he gave to her."

"So the pomegranate seed finally cracked a little," said June.

She handed me another sheet from Myra's diary. "I think you should read this other page now," she said.

She placed it in front of me. "This one's got me a bit puzzled," she said. "It seems as though Myra is retelling some Indian story she's remembered from her younger days. The names sound like they could be Hindu, I think."

This one seemed to start in the middle of a sentence, so I surmised that the beginning of it was missing. I've reproduced what was left of it here. It was also in the style of Myra's coded story and I felt enormously excited and exhilarated as I recognised this and began to read it. This is how the page in front of me began.

was to know the full story of Soma and Senga.

I believe the story starts a long time ago – probably in a foreign country although I cannot be sure of that. I think that Soma loved Senga but she did not return his love because she loved another. For this, Soma vowed revenge.

Soma did not understand that by taking his revenge on them, as well as harming Senga and her lover he would also be harming himself. He did not know that revenge is a weapon that sooner or later turns itself against its user.

He who seeks revenge should know that the only thing he destroys is himself.

To try to forget Senga, Soma went a long way off, to another country, but he could not forget her, even there. The treasure he had stolen stayed hidden, just as his love for her stayed hidden in his heart.

That was the end of the page and all there was of the story. June was right. It was written in the style of what could have been the re-telling in English of a traditional Indian story of some kind.

But I knew immediately what it was.

"June," I said. "Look at those names you thought might be Indian names. Hindu, you called them." I pointed at the first one, Soma. "Spell it backwards," I said. June did so.

"Oh my goodness," she gasped. Then she spelled the other name backwards.

"I can't believe it!" she exclaimed. "Myra is writing her own story! And she's concealed it so that anyone who might happen to pick up her diary and read it, wouldn't recognise it."

"A successful camouflage job," I replied. "And that's how these pages survived, when others didn't."

June and I looked at each other. A real sense of the great-grandmother we shared seemed to be with us in the room. It was almost as though her story had put a spell on us, that neither of us wanted to escape from.

It was June who spoke first. "I've always been proud of the woman Agnes was," she said, "but until now I didn't know enough about Myra, my other great-grandmother, to appreciate who and what she was."

"She was a great soul," I said simply.

That wasn't the sort of thing I ever thought I would say about anyone, but I said it involuntarily, almost as though the words were already harbored in my mind and they just let themselves out because they had to be heard.

As we sat there together, a sense of peace come over me. It was almost as though an old wound had been healed, or an old burden discarded.

June was gathering together the pieces of Myra's diary that she had laid out. "This diary is a treasure," she said, "and I'll put it safely away as a memory of the great-grandmother we never really knew until now."

"Did you notice how Myra used that word, treasure?" I asked her, as she collected the pages.

"Yes, she said something about treasure that he – Amos, as we know she meant – had stolen. But she didn't say who he'd stolen it from."

"Or what it was," I added.

"Or do we know whether it existed at all," said June. "That's what Muriel thinks, that it's just a story with nothing at the base of it."

"Every story starts from somewhere," I said. "even though the way it ends might be very different from how it started."

"So you think that what the family have always referred to as Amos's treasure might have really existed," said June.

"I'm sure that something that Amos treasured did exist," I said, "and no-one has ever found out what it was."

June thought for awhile. Then she said, "I know that when Amos died in 1888, nothing of that sort was discovered amongst his personal effects." She paused. "I also remember being told that the hotel was thoroughly searched by my grandfather when he did the additions and had the balcony built along the front. So that's why I'm dubious about the existence of anything that could be called treasure."

With a feeling of absolute certainty, I replied. What I said was, "it was a treasure to Amos. It existed then, and it exists now. And it's still waiting to be found, somewhere in this hotel."

June looked at me. "How can you be so certain?" she asked.

I didn't know what to reply to that, but from somewhere inside me an explanation came, which was as puzzling to me as it seemed to be to June.

"Bad deeds can live on until they're corrected," was what I said.

There was silence for awhile, then June said "So you think that somewhere here, there is a wrong that still has to be righted."

"That's what something seems to be telling me," I said.

June thought for awhile. "I can't imagine what that could possibly be," she said.

"We don't have to imagine," I replied. "Whatever it was, it is going to come to light soon."

That was when Ralph came bursting into the office. "I've spoken to Jayden," he told us, "and he and Troy are prepared to start on the job immediately. They'll be here this afternoon to give us a quote."

That dispelled the contemplative atmosphere that June and I had been enjoying and returned us to practicalities.

"They'll want access to No.1," said June to me. "Come along, we'll find you another room and move you into it."

It only took me a few minutes to gather my things together but as I closed the door of No.1 behind me, something in my mind seemed to say 'you'll be back here tomorrow – and then we'll know.'

I'd had so many strange and unexpected insights here at the Royal Hotel that I just accepted this as another one and followed June down the corridor as she led me to my substitute room.

"Yes," I thought. "Tomorrow – we'll know."

CHAPTER 11

We find what Amos treasured

I don't know why the change of rooms made it difficult for me to sleep that night but it did. I woke early after a lot of dreams, the details of which I couldn't remember. All I knew was that they were unpleasant and I was glad to get up and have a shower in the antique bathroom.

June was on duty as usual at the door of the dining room and as I went in, she said, "there's a real buzz in the kitchen this morning. I think they're already getting set for our expanded meal offer. Instead of the usual, how would you like eggs benedict today?"

"Sounds great," I said. And it was.

It was about half past seven when a considerable amount of tramping up and down the stairs indicated the arrival of the builders, Troy and Jayden. Ralph appeared as well and it seemed that he'd already approved the layout for the two en-suites so work commenced immediately.

Down in the lounge, where I went after breakfast, I could hear the shouted conversations going on upstairs. Jayden, the carpenter of the two, seemed to be the one in charge.

"What we've gotta do, mate," he was telling Ralph, "is before I get on with puttin' in a new door from No.2 into its en-suite, I'll take up these floorboards so's Troy can get his pipes in. I've ordered all the new fixtures, they'll be here by special delivery tomorrow. Then we'll get everything installed, and Bob's yer uncle."

I really hoped that they wouldn't be replacing Myra's bath, with its antique clawed feet, with a modern one, but I thought better of intruding into the scene to ask. Instead, I went for a walk out into the back garden – Myra's garden – and sat down on her bench to think about what I should do next.

It seemed clear that once the hotel renovations were underway, as they already were, there was no further reason for me to stay in Murrendebri. In any case, I was due back at work at the beginning of next week. However much I wanted to stay here with June, these were the inescapable facts and I was going to have to accept them.

As I was sitting there wondering how I might be able to work out a possible alternative, June came hurrying out towards me.

"What's happened?" I asked. She was definitely excited about something.

"Roger," she said, putting her hand on my arm, "I think you should come upstairs. Ralph has just told me that the building guys have found something that was under the floorboards."

It was a curious moment. I knew that something important was about to happen. I can't put it any other way. "Let's go up," I said, taking her hand; and, hand in hand, for the first time ever, we went inside and up the stairs to where the work was going on.

Ralph met us at the top of the stairs. In his hands he was holding an old wooden box, the sort that maybe would have been used originally to deliver a bottle of port wine. It was very dusty and a few cobwebs were hanging off it.

"The boys found this under the floor in the corner," he said, "where the new pipes have to go through. Jayden said it looked like there might have been a trapdoor there once but it had been nailed up."

"A hiding place," I said.

"A hiding place for treasure, do you think?" asked June.

"Yes. For Amos's treasure," I said. "Whatever it is,

I knew it would be here somewhere."

"It's not very big," Ralph observed.

"It mightn't be big in size," I replied, "but for Amos, it would have been big in significance. I'm certain of that."

"What will we do with it?" Ralph asked. "Open it?"

"Well, that's the only way to find out what it is," said June. "How can we get the top off?"

"Jayden can give us a hand," said Ralph, and he called out, "Hey, Jayden! Bring us your claw hammer, will you mate?"

Jayden was there immediately, and so was Troy. "Put it on my trestle," Jayden said, pointing at his moveable carpenter's bench that he had set up to do his work on. "That way, anything falls out, it won't get lost."

I had to smile to myself – with all the talk about treasure that had been going on, Jayden was obviously expecting a collection of old coins or something like that.

I had my thoughts about what was likely to be in the box – but even I got a surprise when the top came off and the first item was revealed. It was a big plain brown paper envelope. From it, Ralph drew out just one sheet of paper, covered with handwriting. But the minute I saw it, I immediately recognised who had written it. The handwriting was Myra's.

I looked at June. There was no need for us to speak – here was the proof we had suspected. After Myra's death, Amos had rifled through her diary and removed certain pages. Undoubtedly, pages that might have contained perhaps unfavourable references to himself. But if that were the case, why was this one here, in the box of what we suspected was Amos's private treasure trove?

"June," I said, "can you read it out to us?"

She took the page, looked at it, and said "the writing is very small but I'll try." She began to read. This is what it said.

Wednesday 18th

Daddy has summoned me to preside over tiffin tomorrow. He has finally invited Mr Chevally to meet me. What should I make of this?

It seems that Daddy has at last agreed to allow Nina to be courted by Lieutenant Chambers, as she has so long desired. And so it is left to me to be matched with Mr Chevally. Despite Daddy's expressed opinion that he is, as Daddy puts it, 'not one of us'.

What does it mean, to be 'not one of us'? If it were to mean being free of the prejudices that so benight Daddy's view of the world, perhaps it is to be preferred. We will see.

Thursday 19th

Mr Chevally was well presented, courteous, and I

thought acquitted himself well. He is a good-looking man, ambitious and I would say, open to any opportunity to improve his life. As he seems to have done, with his liquor operation of which Daddy so much approves. Perhaps, after all, it may be possible to find some common ground upon which to form a relationship. Time will tell. Hope for better things will always remain my unseen helper.

As I listened to June read this in her clear, steady voice, I felt what seemed like a veil of sadness fall over me. Sadness for Myra – already working towards trying to create a successful marriage out of what today would be a completely untenable situation – but for Amos too. How desperate he must have been for approval, I thought – the elder son outshone by his more personable and talented younger brother, and outdone by him in gaining the affection of the girl he must have fallen in love with. Making what career he could for himself in a foreign country and now, on the point of becoming involved with Myra in what must have been a second-best situation for both of them.

No-one said anything as June handed Myra's page back to Ralph. He put it back in the envelope in which Amos had secreted it so long ago. I think we were all moved by the poignancy of what Myra's brief diary entry had revealed.

But now Ralph was exploring the box, and drew out what remained there. It was a slim package, bigger than the envelope that had contained Myra's writing, but securely wrapped in the old waxed paper people used to protect things from dampness before plastic was invented. The package was heavily sealed.

"Something important here," he said. He turned the package over in his hands and then handed it to me. "Here," he said. "I opened the first one. You open this."

I took the package into both hands. As I did so I felt a kind of electric thrill pass through me. Ralph had said it was important and I could sense that it was more than important, it was something crucial to the story of the hotel and the family who had lived here.

The package was difficult to open – it had been well and truly secured and the sealing strips were hard to tear away. When I had managed to remove them I found that inside the waxed paper parcel was another parcel – a parcel within a parcel. What was inside was surely a treasured item – for Amos, of course, who had made this concealment so long ago.

The inner parcel was easier to open. Inside were two things. One was another envelope, like the one that had contained Myra's diary page. The other was a small envelope with something hard inside of it. The larger one was unsealed and I opened it.

What came out was an old photograph. It was of a young girl, sitting on a chair with her right cheek resting on her right hand and her left hand resting in her lap. The kind of pose that was staged when studio photography came out, so long ago now.

I held the photograph up for the others to see.

Ralph was the first to comment. "It looks like it could be you, June!" he exclaimed.

"It's Agnes, "June replied.

I had that feeling of absolute certainty again. "A picture of Agnes, which she intended to be given to Seth, but it was never delivered to him – kept instead by Amos, as a reminder of what he had never been able to have," I said.

As I held the photograph up, I could see faded writing on the back of it. "Listen to what Agnes wrote," I said to the others.

Dear One
I am sending you this, to wherever you are in London and wherever they send you beyond, so that even though we cannot be together, my heart is yours and always will be.
Forever yours, Agnes.

The effect of this on all of us was magical. Neither Ralph nor June seemed able to speak and I'm certain that I saw June wipe away a tear. Even Troy the plumber was looking a bit misty eyed.

I seemed to be the only one with anything to say. "This tells us a lot about Amos," I said. "First, he was obsessional. He was never able to get over his obsession with Agnes and what he felt for her remained a torture to him for the rest of his life."

"And," said June, "that would have stopped him

from having a really fulfilling relationship with Myra, the girl he married – no matter how much she tried to initiate it."

"Also," put in Ralph, "I reckon he would have been obsessed with the difference between him and his brother Seth, too. Remember, Seth was a much better horseman."

"Yes," I agreed, "that's what brought him all the way up here to Murrendebri when he came to New South Wales. He couldn't keep away from the rivalry with Seth, and he wanted to feel whatever closeness he could to Agnes – even though she belonged to someone else."

"That would have been something that Myra understood," said June, "and probably explains those missing pages in her diary."

"I think so," I said. "He wouldn't have liked having his inner life exposed. By getting rid of Myra's analysis, he was preserving his fantasy."

"Complicated stuff," remarked Ralph.

"It's just human stuff," said June. "We've all got our own little complications."

"That's certainly true," I said. Somewhere inside of me I seemed to feel a need to say more. "And one of the responsibilities of being human," I could hear myself saying, "is not allowing your own little complications to make big complications for others."

"That just means, being unselfish, doesn't it," said June.

"It means being as self-aware as possible," I said. "And being ready to acknowledge and forgive the imperfections you might find in others, too," I added.

"Something that Amos couldn't do," said June.

I was still holding the opened parcel, with the smaller unopened envelope. An understanding of the whole predicament of Amos's life just seemed to keep pouring out of me.

"What Amos couldn't do," I said, "was that he couldn't forgive himself. He couldn't forgive himself for all the bad things he brought into the lives of Seth and Agnes — things that they were able to counteract because of their love for each other. But which he couldn't eliminate from his own life."

"But surely," said June, "he wouldn't have intended to be bad. I don't believe that people are naturally bad. It's what happens to them that makes them do bad things."

"People can fall victims to their own inadequacies," I said. "That is why it's up to every one of us to identify not only our strengths, but our weaknesses as well, and to act from our strengths, rather than risk failing in life because it might be easier to act from our weaknesses. Because," I said, "acting from a weakness not only makes us less viable as human beings, it also jeopardises the people around us who may be dependent on us. So we not only let ourselves down, we let others down too."

It was an unusually big speech for me to make, but I found that I still had more to say.

"It can be a pretty hard thing to do, to identify your own weakness," said Ralph.

"That's the difficulty that the thing they call temptation thrives on," I said. "Tempters like that squire whatsisname that Knottle told us about, who tried to use Amos by giving him an easy way to marry Agnes – the thought of what he'd been offered blotted out all the consequences that were to be felt by his brother Seth. Amos never took those into consideration before he acted."

"Yes," said June. "Amos must have really fallen for the squire's underhand scheme. That was a real weakness."

I was holding the unopened envelope in my hand, and felt that now was the time to open it.

"The final bit of Amos's treasure," I said, as I withdrew from the envelope a tiny item wrapped in a piece of cotton and tied with a small ribbon that had once been white.

I undid the ribbon and opened the tiny parcel. There in the palm of my hand lay a plain golden ring.

I knew immediately what it was but I couldn't prevent my professional self asserting itself.

"Fifteen carat gold," I said, as I peered at the inside of the ring. "Made in Birmingham, according to these marks."

"Yes, but why —" said Ralph.

"The ring that Amos intended for Agnes's fourth finger," I said.

As I said that, a wave of overwhelming feelings coursed through me. It was as though everything that Amos had felt all those years ago still lay somewhere inside me, activated by the sight of what he had intended to be Agnes's wedding ring. I felt the desire, the sense of complicity, the guilt that came with the betrayal of his brother, and the angry frustration when the plan he had agreed to had come to nothing. In a way that I can't find any other way of describing, I felt that I had become a reflection of Amos — or even, in a mysterious kind of way, Amos himself.

"Are you all right, Roger?" I heard Ralph say. That brought me back to earth.

I looked at June and saw her concern This was no time to do anything but capture the moment. As our eyes met I felt a flood of confidence cascade through my veins. My heart raced.

"June," I said, "you know I love you. If you can feel it in your heart to love me, will you marry me?"

As I gazed deeply into her eyes, I could already see her answer.

"Yes," she said. "Roger – I will."

As June and I shared our first real embrace, Ralph looked on as though thunderstruck, and I remember Troy and Jayden capering about and hugging each other as though they shared a part of our story.

The hotel renovations were finished in a week, I drove back to Sydney and arranged to take two more weeks of my accumulated leave, starting from the date June had set for our wedding.

CHAPTER 12

A wedding at Melon Flats

It never occurred to me that when people marry each other, a huge amount of organisation seems to be needed. I mean, I'd known people who'd got married, but I'd never actually been asked to attend any of their weddings and the amount of things that apparently had to be done was a real surprise.

It was inevitable, I suppose, that when Muriel heard that June and I were getting married, she quickly inserted herself into the role of chief organiser. She'd zoomed down from Willow Vale the afternoon before I left for Sydney and confronted us in the hotel office.

"Has he given you a ring?" was her first question, addressed of course to June, who laughed. "Just a moment," she said, opening a drawer in her desk. She drew out the ring I'd seen that first day just after we'd met – I'd thought of it as the commercial traveller discourager. She handed it to me and held out her hand. I slipped the ring onto her finger, and she held up her hand for Muriel's inspection. "He has now," she said.

With that settled, Muriel busied herself with the next matter.

"You'll be having a white wedding, of course," she announced. "Who have you got making your frock."

"Well," said June, "I rather thought I would wear my mother's wedding dress, which she kept – she showed it to me before she died, and I'd like to wear it in memory of her."

Muriel's expression showed that she was not entirely pleased with this decision but she passed over it with no comment, other than the advice to make sure the dress was sent to a reliable dry cleaner first.

Now it was my turn for interrogation. Looking me up and down, Muriel embarked on her first line of attack. "Who is your Best Man," she barked.

"My what?" I said, I'd never heard of Best Men, whoever they were, and was really quite stumped for an answer.

"I thought as much," Muriel crowed, "no idea of what your responsibilities are. Obviously you'll need to be Taken In Hand."

I was surprised that I didn't feel the enmity that this statement had stirred in me the last time Muriel had threatened me with it. The situation was quickly raised above confrontational level by June, who said – to me – "why, Ralph would be the obvious choice. He'd be delighted. We can ask him later."

Muriel wasn't scoring many points but she now played what turned out to be her trump card. "A morning wedding, I think you said," she observed, and June nodded. Muriel turned her attention to me again.

"Eleven a.m.," she announced. "What do you intend to wear."

Well, I have to say, I'd never given this matter a moment's thought. But I found an immediate answer.

"I have recently purchased," I said to Muriel, "a quite expensive tweed jacket. I think that should –" I got no further.

"What!" exclaimed Muriel, in a ferocious display of displeasure. "What! That awful Harris tweed thing you wore to the races! What an unbelievable suggestion."

Strangely, an air of amelioration now seemed to flood into Muriel's attitude. She turned away from me and beamed at June.

"He'll need a full morning suit and top hat," she informed June, "and so will Ralph. That's assuming he's going to be the Best Man," she said in my direction. "And suitable gloves," she added, giving both of us the benefit of her approval.

"But," June attempted to say, "we thought just something simple —" she got no further.

"Simple!" roared Muriel. "The union of two Chevally descendants and you want it to be simple! You do realise, the whole district will be looking on. We mustn't let the side down."

Oddly, this statement from Muriel, which seemed to indicate that the Seth/Amos divide had been replaced in her mind by a unified family outlook, gave me an unexpectedly warm feeling. I reached out to Muriel and gave her hand a squeeze.

"Whatever you say, Muriel," I said. "Although," I added, "I've got no idea where I'll get all this morning clobber from."

"Hired," she replied succinctly. "I'll give you the details and you can bring it all up from Sydney." A look of pleasant nostalgia flitted across her face. "It's a very reliable firm," she said, "that I used to hire a morning suit for Phineas, when we had the Royal Visit up here a few years ago."

It was very difficult not to gape open-mouthed at the thought of Knottle, not only wearing whatever a morning suit turned out to be, complete with a top hat, and suitable gloves, participating in a Royal Visit, but Muriel left no time to speculate as she moved on to what was clearly the most important item on her agenda.

"Now," she said to June, having obviously finished

with me, "we have to deal with the question of Who Will Give You Away."

"Give her away?" I gasped. But this did nothing to halt the progress of Muriel's already determined plan.

"Normally," she explained, "it would be your senior male relative."

"Oh," said June, "then perhaps Harry —"

"Definitely not," interrupted Muriel. "Harry's function will be to host your reception at the homestead, starting precisely at 1p.m. He's already agreed."

"Oh! but —" June said, but she got no further.

"These days," Muriel announced, "times have changed. Sexism has been thrown out of the window like old dishwater. As one of your senior relations in the direct line, I will give you away myself."

Both June and I agreed later that it would have been unproductive to try and debate this pronouncement. Our modest little wedding ceremony in the Melon Flats Community Church, near where the recent family reunion had been held, had been hijacked by Matron Muriel Chevally and the only thing to do, as I said to June, was to go with the flow.

So, in short, that's what we did. Yes, I hired the morning outfit decreed by Muriel and even though it made me feel like a prize galah, wore it for the ceremony. The beautiful sight of June coming up the short aisle towards me, even though she was propelled by Muriel, was a sight I'll never forget. The church was crammed full of relatives, there were even people standing at the entrance because all the pews were full.

Afterwards, up at the Melon Creek homestead, Harry's family had put on what Muriel insisted on calling a Wedding Breakfast, even though we were having it at lunchtime. There was roast beef accompanied, of course, by a glass or two of sparkling shiraz and then June and I had to cut the wedding cake.

Soon the festivities were over. June and I left for our honeymoon which we spent in Tasmania, taking the opportunity to visit MONA, the Museum of Old and New Art in Hobart. June loved this and on the advice of one of the curators there, when we got back to Sydney she enrolled as a student in the National Art School, where she is still studying for her chosen career as an artist. And, needless to say, we're living in our house in Balmain – from where I'd once set out for Melon Flats, to find the mysterious family I didn't know I had.

And ended finding the mysterious treasure concealed by my sad and sorry great-grandfather, but for me, the real treasure of a lifetime – June.

Lightning Source UK Ltd.
Milton Keynes UK
UKHW020632101022
410232UK00015B/844